SPOTLIGHT
rint of Simon & Schuster Children's Publishing Division
venue of the Americas, New York, New York 10020
non Spotlight edition August 2014
by Simon & Schuster, Inc. All rights reserved, including the right of
ction in whole or in part in any form.
SPOTLIGHT and colophon are registered trademarks of
& Schuster, Inc.
Sarah Albee
rt by Anthony VanArsdale
d by Ciara Gay
rmation about special discounts for bulk purchases, please contact
& Schuster Special Sales at 1-866-506-1949
ess@simonandschuster.com.
ctured in the United States of America 0714 FFG
7 6 5 4 3 2 1
8-1-4814-1652-8 (pbk)
8-1-4814-1653-5 (hc)
8-1-4814-1654-2 (eBook)
of Congress Catalog Card Number 2013955431

Double or Not

by Belle Payton

Simon Spotlight

New York   London   Toronto   Sydne

SIMON
An imp
1230 A
This Si
© 2014
reprodu
SIMON
Simon
Text by
Cover a
Design
For inf
Simon
or busi
Manufa
10 9 8
ISBN 9
ISBN 9
ISBN 9
Library

This b
places
of the
living

CHAPTER ONE

"Alex?"

No answer.

"Alex?"

Not so much as a twitch. Ava took a step into the room. The shades were up, but it was still dim and shadowy in her sister's bedroom, as the September sun had not yet risen.

"Al!"

Alex, a lump beneath the gray covers, mumbled something Ava couldn't hear and turned her back to her sister.

Desperate times called for desperate measures. Ava strode in and sat down heavily on her twin's bed, causing the lump under the covers to give a little bounce. Then she pulled the pillow out from under her sleeping sister's head.

Alex sat up, her long, curly hair wild, her hands groping blindly. "What? What! Time to get up! What day is it?" A second later, her eyes focused on Ava. Her expression turned from sleepy confusion to wide-awake panic. "Ava!" she whispered, throwing back the covers. "Did I oversleep?"

Ava stood up. She was glad Alex wasn't sick or anything, but this was still weird: Alex never overslept. She was always the first one up; annoyingly chipper in the morning, to the dismay of Ava, who was not a morning person, and their older brother Tommy, who wasn't either.

"Yes, but you're not going to be late," said Ava. "We have plenty of time before the bus comes."

"Plenty of time!" repeated Alex as she flew to her chair and grabbed the clothes she'd laid out the night before. "Twenty minutes is not 'plenty of time.'" She headed toward the bathroom. "How could I have overslept today, of all days! I have seventy-eight signatures, and I still need twenty-two more by the end of the day."

"Relax, Al," said Ava. "Just don't spend

nineteen minutes on your hair today and you'll be fine."

Ava heard her twin grunt and slam the door to the bathroom, which was between their bedrooms. A second later, she heard the shower going.

Ava stood and contemplated her sister's neat-as-a-pin bedroom, now bathed in pinky-gold tones as the sun rose in the eastern sky. Alex's clipboard was on the top of the tidy pile of books on her desk. She was running for seventh-grade class president at Ashland Middle School, and campaign petitions were due today. But today was a big day for both of them; she, Ava, had slept fitfully all night long and finally gotten up before her alarm had rung. This afternoon was the first day of football tryouts, and she was a combination of excited and nervous.

The kitchen was bustling when Ava entered. Coach Sackett had his orange Ashland Tigers hat on, his briefcase was near the door, and he had just finished packing the girls' lunches. Mrs. Sackett was still in her workout clothes—an oversize Patriots T-shirt and yoga pants—her long, curly hair pulled back into a ponytail. She had just come back from walking Moxy, the

Sacketts' Australian shepherd. Tommy's mouth was full—a common occurrence—as he downed what remained of his bacon, egg, and cheese sandwich and stood up from the table.

"Alex overslept," announced Ava.

Coach froze in mid-swig of his coffee.

Tommy stopped chewing.

Mrs. Sackett stood, holding Moxy's food dish.

They all gaped at Ava.

"Wow. Alex overslept?" asked Tommy.

"Is she feeling sick?" asked Mrs. Sackett. Moxy thumped her tail loudly on the kitchen floor, waiting for Mrs. Sackett to set the bowl down.

"Nope, she's fine," said Ava, pouring out her cereal. "She was probably up late texting with Emily about her campaign strategy."

Coach grabbed his briefcase, pecked Mrs. Sackett good-bye on the cheek, and leaned across the table to ruffle Ava's already-mussed-up hair.

"Hey, careful there, Coach. I worked hard on my hairstyle this morning," said Ava. She twirled a piece of short, curly brown hair around her finger and laughed.

"Good luck at tryouts today, darlin'," he said,

heading for the door. "Remember to stay low and move those feet."

Ava grinned. "I will, Coach. I will." Was his Texas accent re-emerging? He had grown up near Ashland but had lived in the Northeast for most of his adult life. They'd been back in Texas for several weeks now, and Ava was starting to detect an accent creeping back into his voice. Subtle stuff—like dropping the *g*'s on his *–ing* word endings. She made a mental note to ask Alex if she had noticed this too.

Alex hurried into the kitchen just after Tommy and Coach had backed out of the driveway and driven away. Her expression was frazzled, but the rest of her looked as smooth and put-to-gether as ever. "Mom, no time for breakfast," she said, picking up her lunch and swinging her backpack onto her shoulder. "I need to get to the bus stop in time to plan my strategy. I need seventh graders to sign my clipboard."

Mrs. Sackett handed Alex a piece of toast and a peeled banana on a paper towel and nodded. She probably knew there was no arguing with Alex about the importance of a good breakfast on a day like today. "Good luck today, girls," she said, as the sisters traipsed to the door, laden down with heavy backpacks. "It's a big day for both of you."

And out they went.

"Al, you know there are only four kids at our stop, and three are in sixth grade and one is in eighth," said Ava, huffing along beside her sister toward the bus stop just around the corner. For someone who hated sports, Alex could certainly walk fast!

Alex nodded, finished her toast, swallowed the last of the banana, and brushed the crumbs off her shirt, all while maintaining her break-neck pace. As they turned the corner, they could see the bus in the distance, making a stop at the far end of the street. "I know," she said. "But I think a couple of the kids two stops after us are in seventh. It can't hurt to ask."

"Speaking of asking, were you going to ask me how I was feeling about today?" asked Ava.

The bus was approaching their stop, and Alex had joined the little line of kids waiting to board. She turned and looked at her sister quizzically. "You? Why would you be stressing about me getting twenty-two more signatures? You never worry about details like that."

Ava rolled her eyes as the bus doors opened.

She followed Alex up the steep steps and said good morning to Mrs. Fogarty, their bus driver. "I meant how I was feeling about football. Which starts today, as you've obviously forgotten."

"Oh. Right," said Alex, and she slid into their usual seat midway down on the right. "You're still absolutely positive you want to try out?"

Ava glared at her. "I'm a good kicker. Coach and Tommy both say I am. Why shouldn't I try out for the team?"

"Because we're in Texas," said Alex patiently, with the air of someone who has explained the same point many times before. "And they do things differently here. What if they say girls can't try out? Are you going to make a big fuss about it?"

"They're not going to," said Ava, hoping if she said it convincingly it would turn out to be the truth. "I looked up the rules on the district sports website, and there's nothing on there that says girls can't play."

"Probably because the situation has never arisen," Alex mused. "And it's doubly compli-cated, of course, because of who our dad is. If you do make the team, how will you know if it was based on your talent or if it's because our dad is the coach of the Ashland Tigers?"

"Wow," said Ava, her voice dripping with hurt and sarcasm. "Thanks for the vote of confidence, Al."

"Ava," said Alex, more kindly. "I didn't mean it like that. I just—" She broke off as the brakes squeaked, the bus slowed to a stop, and the doors swung open. "Be right back." Alex jumped to her feet and squeezed past Ava to intercept the three kids making their way down the aisle.

"Hey! Hi!" she said brightly. "Aren't you guys in seventh grade?"

Ava groaned inwardly. She could see Mrs. Fogarty's furrowed brow in the rearview mirror as she waited for Alex and the others to sit down so she could get moving again.

Out the window, Ava could see several cars that had stopped for the bus's flashing red lights, most likely people in a hurry to get to work.

The first kid, a tall girl that Ava vaguely recognized from her Spanish class, blinked at Alex in surprise. "Um, yeah," she said. "I'm in seventh."

"I thought so!" said Alex eagerly. "Would you mind giving me your signature for my candidacy for class president?"

"Find a seat, please, ladies," Mrs. Fogarty called.

The girl probably saw the determination on Alex's face and figured the quickest way to resolve the situation would be to comply. She took the clipboard from Alex and hastily scrawled her name on it. Alex looked like she wanted to blockade the way until the other two could sign, but then Mrs. Fogarty actually half stood, looking extremely annoyed, so Alex quickly squeezed back into her seat beside Ava. "Twenty-one to go," she said, and clicked her pen closed.

CHAPTER TWO

Alex filed off the bus behind Ava. "We're a few minutes early, so I'm going to see if I can get some more signatures. See you at lunch!"

Ava frowned and gave a little shrug, then was swallowed up in the crowd of chattering kids who were gathered around the front of Ashland Middle School.

Alex watched her sister go, feeling troubled. Was Ava mad at her for what she'd said about the football tryouts? Or maybe she wasn't mad at all—just preoccupied and nervous about trying out. Ava was naturally shy, so she was probably not psyched about putting herself in the spotlight. That must be why she hadn't wished

Alex good luck with her signatures.

She spotted a kid she'd met last week at the after-school origami club and made her way over, clipboard at the ready.

The second bell was ringing as Alex hurried into third-period social studies. Her friend Emily Campbell was already sitting at her desk, so Alex had missed out on the pre-class socializing. She slid into her seat next to Emily.

"Where've you been? You're always here early," said Emily, and then, without waiting for Alex to answer, she said, "What a cute shirt!"

"Thanks," said Alex, smoothing down her shirt and then patting her hair into place. Thank goodness she'd shampooed and conditioned it last night, or today might have been a disastrous hair day. "I feel like I just ran a marathon. But I got seven more signatures on my petition last period." She showed Emily her clipboard. "Just fourteen more to go. It's been really hard to nail these last few signatures, because I'm new and I don't know all the seventh graders the way Logan Medina and Ella Sanchez do."

"Logan probably does know everyone, but not Ella," said Emily. "I'm pretty surprised she wants to run for president. It doesn't seem like her thing. She's all about being a brainiac, not Miss Popularity. Anyway, did you try going to some of the after-school clubs like you said you were going to?"

Alex nodded. "I went to the origami club last week. I had to fold about a zillion paper cranes, but I got six signatures, so it was worth it. And I went to Ultimate Frisbee and got hit on the head. That was fine, though, because practically everyone signed out of sympathy, at least those who hadn't signed Logan's petition."

"Logan." Emily rolled her eyes. "He's totally riding the popularity wagon. I don't think he's serious enough to be a good class president."

"Tell that to the ninety percent of the girls in our grade who have a crush on him," said Alex grimly. She stared down at her clipboard. "Where am I going to get fourteen signatures before the end of the day?"

"Maybe you should get yourself a detention," said Emily with a laugh as Mrs. Bridges clapped her hands to get the class's attention. "There's always a ton of kids in there."

At lunchtime Ava found Alex in the cafeteria and observed with annoyance that her sister was still brandishing her dumb clipboard. They had a quick, silent exchange—a twin thing, their mom called it. A creepy twin thing, their brother called it. Whatever it was called, Ava and Alex definitely knew how to communicate with each other without coming right out and speaking, and today they were in silent agreement that they both wanted to sit apart from their usual tables full of chattering friends. Ava led the way to a table in a corner, one that wasn't usually occupied because it was so far away from the serving stations.

"How are your signatures going?" asked Ava, unzipping her lunch bag and pulling out the peanut butter and banana sandwich Coach had made for her. She figured she might as well ask, since that was what Alex was going to talk about anyway.

"Still working on them," said Alex with a sigh. "I just got one on the way here, when a girl dropped her water bottle in the hallway and spilled it. I ran and got paper towels in the bathroom for her, and she was so grateful she signed, even though I think she had been planning to sign Logan's. Look at the guy."

She gestured across the cafeteria with her sandwich.

Ava looked. Logan was perched at the edge of a table full of girls, talking and gesturing animatedly. Every few moments the girls would break into a fit of giggles. "Didn't he read the announcements over the intercom this morning?" Ava asked.

Alex rolled her eyes. "He reads them every chance he gets," she said. "Emily told me he wants to work in Hollywood and be a voice-over guy someday—you know, like the voice that does suspenseful movie previews?"

"He does have a nice voice," admitted Ava. "And that guy next to him—Xander somebody-or-other—came to our homeroom this morning and passed out candy bars that said 'Vote for Logan—A Sweet Deal.'"

Alex looked at Ava in alarm. "He did? That's so sneaky! We're not supposed to put up our posters and start campaigning until tomorrow! We haven't even turned in our petitions!"

Ava shrugged. "I guess he figured he's a shoo-in—Xander was bragging that Logan got his hundred signatures in, like, two days."

"Candy bars," muttered Alex. "Talk about buying votes." Her eyes widened. "Wait. You didn't take one, did you?"

Ava was holding up one of Xander's candy bars. She gave her sister a guilty look and put it down. "I figured if I took one, that would be one less he'd hand out to someone who might actually vote for him," she said. "It was all for the right cause."

"Very noble of you," said Alex dryly. She took a moody bite of her sandwich.

Ava took out her napkin to wipe some peanut butter off her hands and saw that there was something written on it. A message from Coach: *Work ethic, talent, and heart. You've got 'em all, Ava Sackett.* She smiled and leaned down to tuck the napkin into her backpack. She couldn't expect Alex to understand her jitters about tryouts today, but at least Coach did.

"And that's Ella over there," Alex continued.

Ava tuned back in to what her sister was saying.

"She's sitting at the smart-kid table. And I

admit, she's really smart. She's in my science class, plus we're both in debate club and math club. I bet her posters are going to be super fancy. Her dad owns a copy company, which is so not fair."

"Where does the campaign money come from?" asked Ava. "Where does Logan get the funding for candy bars and Ella for fancy posters?"

"That's just it," said Alex. "They say we shouldn't spend more than twenty-five dollars for our campaign, but that's what, like, five posters cost to make. I'm positive they've both already spent way more than that." She sighed and looked down at her clipboard.

"I don't think you should be too worried," said Ava. "They might have fancy campaign stuff, but you're a great public speaker. And you're super organized, and you have great ideas. Just play your game. That's what Coach always says."

Alex nodded and smiled gratefully. "Thanks, Ave. I appreciate your support." But the worried look reappeared on her face. She took a long sip of her milk. Then she started gathering up her lunch stuff. "Sorry to leave you here, but I better get going. I still need thirteen signatures before the end of the day."

As Alex stood up, Ava gave her an expectant look. "Aren't you going to wish me luck?"

Alex looked up from her clipboard, puzzled. "Do you have a test today?"

Ava sighed. "No. Never mind. Go get your signatures."

"Oh, wait, sorry," said Alex, light finally dawning. "Right. Football. Good luck, Ave. Knock 'em dead."

As she left the cafeteria and headed toward English, Alex felt her desperation growing. Where was she going to find the last thirteen signatures? Clearly her two opponents had already gotten their hundred signatures easily. She looked around her at kids heading toward their next class. She thought about stopping people randomly, but she wasn't even positive who was in seventh grade! It really wasn't fair— she was new to the school. She'd already asked the kids in all her classes. Some had signed, but just as many had said they'd already signed for Logan or Ella.

Then a sudden idea struck her. She stopped

short, and a girl who'd been walking behind her bumped into her. The girl's books tumbled to the floor.

"Oh! I'm so sorry!" said Alex, stooping down to help her retrieve them.

"That's okay," said the girl. She stood back up, and Alex handed her the last of her books. "Hey, are you in seventh grade by any chance?" asked Alex eagerly.

The girl shook her head. "Sixth," she said, and went on her way.

But Alex remained undaunted. She was remembering what Emily had jokingly mentioned in homeroom this morning. Detention! Now there was an untapped source of new signatures! It was highly improbable that any kids in detention would be friends of Ella's. All Ella's friends were smart and motivated and would never be caught dead in detention. It was even unlikely that they'd be friends of Logan's. He was a jock, and kids who were serious about sports generally kept themselves out of detention, as coaches were usually displeased if their players missed practice time. Detention would likely be full of what reporters on the news liked to call "undecided voters." In seventh grade, that category would be kids who didn't follow school government very closely, or who didn't even know there was a campaign. The question was, how did one get a detention?

Alex stood outside Ms. Palmer's English classroom and waited for the second bell to ring.

Jack Valdeavano, a friend of hers and Ava's whom Ava played basketball with a lot (and whom Alex was pretty sure Ava had a crush on), paused as he was about to go inside. "Coming?" he asked her.

"Yup. Be right there," said Alex. Her breathing was shallow, and she felt drops of perspiration on her upper lip. She was never late for class. Never. *How late do I have to be to get a detention?* she wondered.

Jack gave her a puzzled look and headed inside.

Thirty seconds later the bell rang. By now Alex was almost in panic mode. She leaned against the locker, breathing hard. A sixth grader sprinted past her at top speed, obviously late for class. She watched him skid to slow down and then disappear out of sight around the corner. Now she was the only one in the hall.

She counted to five, then walked into the classroom.

Ms. Palmer was passing out papers.

"S-s-sorry I'm late!" Alex said in a high, quivering voice, as she slipped into her empty desk next to Megan Schiller.

"Hello, Alex," said Ms. Palmer, putting a paper on Alex's desk. "Nice of you to join us." She smiled and moved on. Alex sighed.

She picked up her paper and peeked at it. It was an essay about the poet Robert Herrick. She'd gotten a ninety-seven and a smiley face.

When she had finished passing out the papers, Ms. Palmer told the class to take out their books. They were reading *Antigone*.

"Um, excuse me, Ms. Palmer?" Alex waved her hand urgently to get Ms. Palmer's attention.

She turned. "Yes, Alex?"

"My book. I forgot my book. I didn't bring it to class." Although her heart was pounding, Alex tried to put a defiant, *who cares* look on her face.

"Oh. Well, never mind. You can look on with Megan today."

Alex glanced at Megan Schiller. Megan flashed her a friendly smile, revealing a mouthful of purple braces.

Alex tried again. "No, but see, I might even have lost it. My book. I might not bring it tomorrow, either. That's really bad, isn't it?"

Ms. Palmer looked at Alex, puzzled. "I'm sure it will turn up, Alex. In the meantime, I have a spare copy you can borrow. You can put your annotations on sticky notes until you find your book."

Alex closed her eyes and blew out a breath. This was not working. What did it take to get a detention around here? Should she threaten to rob a bank or something? "Well, but see, I also might, um, might have to be late for class tomorrow, and I don't think I'll have a note with me."

Her glance flickered over to Jack, who was sitting several seats away. He had an amused grin on his face. Ms. Palmer was staring at Alex over the tops of her glasses with a look of utter incomprehension. It was as though Alex had suddenly switched to speaking in Urdu.

"Alex," she said. "You can look on with Megan. Can we get on with class, please?"

Alex slumped in her chair. "Yes, sorry," she mumbled.

So much for that idea.

She managed to get several more signatures in the hallway between classes, but by the time the last bell had rung, she had just ninety-six—still four short.

Alex stood near the main entrance of the school, just outside the office. Kids were rushing by on their way to catch buses or get changed for sports tryouts, which all began today. She looked glumly down at the ninety-six signatures and felt a lump rise in her throat. Was this where it would end? Would it just be Logan and Ella in the campaign?

Right then Logan Medina emerged from the office and saluted Alex, an impish grin on his handsome face. "Just handed in my signatures," he said to her. "Had them done last week."

In spite of her misery, Alex was struck by his low, resonant voice. It was like melted honey. No wonder girls mooned over the guy.

"Great," snapped Alex. "Good for you."

"See ya around," he said, and gave her a thumbs-up, then joined the throngs of kids heading outside.

"Must not cry," Alex said to herself through gritted teeth. "Presidents don't cry." But she could feel tears of frustration spring to her eyes. Why was she putting herself through this? Logan was going to win, and if he didn't, Ella certainly would. She, Alex, couldn't even get a hundred lousy signatures just to get to the next phase of the campaign.

"Hey, Sackett," said a voice to her right.

Alex quickly rubbed her eyes with the heel of her hand and turned. It was Jack.

"Hey, Jack," she said, her voice a little too high and bright.

"You need a ride home or something? My mom's outside, and we're heading to soccer practice—we go right past your house."

"Oh, no thanks, I'm good," said Alex. "I—I'm waiting for someone."

"Okay, sounds good." He turned to leave.

"I thought soccer was a spring sport in Texas," said Alex.

He turned back. "It is. But those of us who know that soccer is the world's greatest game and a far superior sport to football play for the club team."

Alex smiled. He was nice. No wonder Ava liked him. A thought dawned on Alex. "Hey, Jack? I'm guessing you already signed Logan's petition, right?"

"Logan? That would be a no."

"Oh!" she said, surprised. "I assumed because you were a—because you were athletic you would have signed his. I thought he had the athlete vote."

"Nope," said Jack simply. "I haven't been following our class government all that closely, to be honest. But I'll sign your petition if you want." He grinned and held out his hand for her pen and clipboard, and scribbled down his name. Then he looked more closely. "You've got ninety-seven signatures. How many do you need?"

"Three more," she said miserably. "But I have no one left to ask, and they have to be in by three thirty. I was planning to try the kids in detention, but it fell through." She felt the tears well up in her eyes again.

Jack stared at her. A grin spread across his face, but he quickly suppressed it. "Is that why you came in late to English today? And why you didn't bring your book? You were trying to get Palmer to give you a detention?"

Alex nodded sadly. "I couldn't even get her to yell at me."

Now Jack laughed heartily. "This is your lucky day," he said, taking her by the elbow and propelling her toward the front door. "Because it's only three seventeen, and I have three friends sitting in my mom's car, and I bet they won't mind signing your petition one bit. They probably don't even know there is an election, they're such lame citizens."

Alex felt a strong urge to throw her arms around Jack's neck. As it was probably not the best thing to do on several levels, she restrained herself. But she followed Jack out the door.

Two minutes later she was dashing back inside to file her signatures in the front office.

CHAPTER THREE

Ava sat on a bench in the girls' locker room, her heart thumping hard in her chest as she laced up her cleats. All around her, girls were changing into sports clothes, chattering cheerfully with one another. She was relieved not to see anyone she knew, at least not well. There was a girl from her social studies class near her, and judging from her tennis shoes and knee pads, Ava guessed she was trying out for volleyball.

"Hi!" the girl said. "What sport are you trying out for?"

Ava mumbled, "Football" under her breath.

"Sorry, what? Did you say cross-country?"

"No, football," Ava replied.

"Volleyball?"

"Football!" said Ava loudly.

The chattering in the locker room stopped. It was as though someone had flicked off a radio.

"Football?" the girl repeated. "Like, as in, the football team?"

Ava nodded, staring down at the floor. She could hear someone whispering, and then the chattering resumed. But she sensed a different energy in the air. Was it shock? Amazement? Disapproval? She couldn't tell. She didn't feel like finding out. She grabbed her water bottle, slammed her locker closed, and headed out toward the football field.

The notice on the school's athletic page had said no pads or helmets for the first day, and Ava was glad. Today would be largely conditioning, she assumed, and she was good at that stuff. Ever since the day when she was about three and begged her dad to show her how to throw and catch a football, it was clear to her family that she had inherited the Sackett athletic gene.

When she got to the field, she saw a cluster of guys standing near the twenty yard line, and more emerging from the boys' locker room and joining the growing throng. Mr. Kenerson was near the bleacher area, conferring with his four assistant coaches. Ava didn't recognize the assistants, who wore similar white polo shirts, visors, and mirrored sunglasses. One of them was vigorously chewing gum. They were all staring down at Coach Kenerson's clipboard and didn't see her approach.

The boys did, though. Their loud chattering, laughing, friendly pushing, and general kidding around suddenly stopped as she approached the group.

Ava figured she might as well say something. "Hi," she said, as brightly and cheerfully as she could.

A few guys murmured hello, and then silence ensued.

She scanned the group, looking for a friendly face. Where was her friend Corey? He didn't seem to have come out of the locker room yet. She recognized Logan Medina, the kid running against Alex for president, and his friend Xander. Next to Xander was Andy Baker, a kid from her social studies class. She saw Xander whisper something to Andy. Andy looked at her and snickered. She tried to ignore them, and glanced around to see if the coaches had noticed her yet.

They had. All five of them stood motionless, as though they'd been frozen with a supervillain's freeze-ray gun. The coach who'd been chewing gum seemed to have swallowed it.

Ava's heart sank. Why was everyone acting so surprised to see her? She'd signed up for football at the Activities Fair. The boys were staring at her like she'd just sprouted a second head or something. Maybe they hadn't thought she was serious.

"Are you looking for cross-country?" someone behind Ava asked. She turned.

It was Xander.

Ava's anger flared, but she didn't let him see. "No. Football," she said.

"I hear she's good," said another voice. She turned. It was Corey.

He didn't smile at her, but she detected a friendly twinkle in his eye. She told him thank-you with her eyes. She knew better than to be too friendly to him—it could make it awkward for him if it turned out she stunk. She would have to prove herself by the way she played, rather than with words.

Coach Kenerson approached the group. Ava couldn't see his eyes behind his mirrored sunglasses, but she could tell he was looking straight at her.

He stopped a few feet from them and pointed at her. "Sackett, isn't it?"

Ava nodded, almost imperceptibly.

"Step over here a minute, will you?"

He turned before she could respond. She trotted after him, trying to catch up to his long strides. He stopped when they were out of earshot of the rest of the group.

"I saw that you were on the sign-up sheet. I have to say I was pretty surprised. Are you here to try out?" he asked her. His tone wasn't mean, exactly. *More . . . skeptical,* Ava thought.

"Um, yes," she said.

"You know this is tackle football, right?"

"Yes."

"Are you familiar with how the game is played?"

"Yes, of course."

He pulled off his sunglasses and squinted down at her. "From what I've observed, Sackett, you don't strike me as much of a football fan, let alone a player. No offense."

Ava blinked up at him. "Sorry? I'm not sure—"

"Why, just yesterday morning, I was talking

about pass protection, and you thought I was talking about ways students could protect their hall passes."

"I—I did?"

"And this morning, when someone brought up what a great rusher Tyler Whitley is, you asked why it would be beneficial to rush through an assessment."

That was when she realized what was going on. "Oh, no, that wasn't me," she said. "I think maybe you mean my sister, Alex. She's in your homeroom. We're identical twins. And she— ah—she doesn't really follow the game very closely."

He took a step backward, as though the news had struck him in the chest.

"Identical twins," he repeated.

"Yes."

He considered this. "Well, be that as it may, I have to tell you something, Sackett," he said. "I'm really not sure whether our district rules allow this."

Ava's anger flared again, which made her bolder. "Allow what, Coach?" She was going to make him say it.

He put his sunglasses back on, and then took

them off again and cleaned them on his pant leg. He seemed flustered. "Well, uh, allow people— uh, people like you, to play."

"You mean girls?" She crossed her arms.

Now he looked really uncomfortable. He looked from side to side as though hoping someone might suddenly appear and help him out with this conversation. When no one did, he said, "Well, yes. That's it. Allow girls. I've been coaching eighteen years and have never had to deal with this."

"Well, Coach K, with all due respect," said Ava, choosing her words carefully, "I checked the rules on the district's website. I didn't see anything that said girls aren't allowed to play."

He grumbled. "That doesn't mean much, Sackett. The website can't cover every contingency. I imagine it doesn't say, 'Texas longhorn cattle are also prohibited from playing,' but that doesn't mean we would let one play if it were to show up." He chuckled at his own joke and then went back to looking stern.

"I used to play on the local Pee Wee team in my old town in Massachusetts, and being a girl was never an issue there," Ava said. She was start- ing to get tired of arguing with Coach K—she wasn't used to having to defend herself so strenuously.

Luckily, Coach Kenerson gave a little grunt and said, "All right, we'll proceed for now. It's all drills and conditioning, no contact. You can join us today, and tonight I'll make some calls to the athletic director and the district and get this all sorted out."

"Okay. Thanks, Coach," said Ava.

"But Sackett, don't expect any special treatment just because of your last name, or because you're a—a girl. You got that?"

She grinned at that. "I got it, Coach. I plan to earn my spot on this team same as everyone else."

He nodded, and she caught a hint of an approving look on his gruff face.

He blew his whistle. "Captains!" he bellowed. "Two laps around, and then line 'em up for team calisthenics!"

The two captains, eighth graders whom Ava didn't know, led the fifty or so kids toward the fence that surrounded the area around the football field and began jogging. Ava was happy to do something she felt confident about. She was in pretty good shape, thanks to all the working out she'd done with Tommy and the pickup basketball she'd been playing at the park near her house.

They were rounding the far corner of the field when Ava felt someone kick the sole of her right cleat. The ground rushed toward her and she came very close to landing on her nose. But somehow, her right foot managed to find the ground in front of her, and she maintained her footing, waving her arms awkwardly.

"Oh, sorry about that, Sackett," said Andy Baker. "My bad."

He pulled ahead of her and kept running.

Ava wanted to believe he hadn't meant to do it, but she wasn't totally sure. She came in last.

When Ava finally joined the team, the captains ordered everyone to form three lines. As Ava chose the middle line, she heard someone say, "Hey, Sackett."

She looked. It was Xander.

"Back line for rookies," he said. "It's a thing."

She opened her mouth to say something, and then closed it. Without a word, she moved back to the third line, between two skinny sixth graders. But her temper was simmering.

After the team warm-ups, Coach Kenerson

called them in to take a knee. He introduced the assistant coaches. Ava knew she wouldn't remember their names and hoped there'd be a handout. But she tried to study their faces so she'd remember who was offensive coordinator, defensive coordinator, lineman coach, receivers and quarterback coach, and running backs coach. *Where would a kicker go?* she wondered.

"After practice, there will be a sign-up in the"—he stopped and cleared his throat—"outside the locker room."

Ava knew it was because of her. *Well, so what?* she thought fiercely.

"I'd like you to sign your name next to the position or positions you're trying out for," he continued. "Think outside the box, please. I realize most of you want to be either quarterback or wide receiver, but remember, it takes all positions to make a great team."

The boys murmured to one another and then quieted back down.

"We're not going to break down into positions just yet," said Coach K. "Today is going to be drills, testing, and conditioning. Be ready to run some more, fellas."

Ava felt several dozen pairs of eyes turn to

look at her. She felt her face burning, but she kept a neutral expression.

Then Coach K blew his whistle and divided everyone up into six stations for the drills, and the practice began.

CHAPTER FOUR

"Sackett! A moment, please."

Practice had just ended. Ava was doubled over, trying to catch her breath. So was everyone else, though—at least she wasn't the only one. She stood up, and the world tilted one way, then the other. She knew her hair was spiky with sweat, and her face must be red as a berry, which was what usually happened after a tough workout, and this had been tough. She hadn't had a single opportunity to do any kicking, though. How was she supposed to try out to be a kicker if they hadn't kicked?

Instead they'd gone through a series of physical tests: the forty-yard dash, sprints up and down the field the long way, shuttle runs from one sideline to the other, running forward, backward, forward, and backward, until the ground beneath Ava's feet seemed to roll like an ocean wave and she saw stars all around her. They'd done something the coaches called the pro-agility test, which involved sliding side to side from one cone to another. She'd remembered what her dad had told her about keeping low and staying balanced on the balls of her feet, and she'd been pretty happy with how she'd done. She'd beaten the kid she'd been partnered with on the drill, and although she knew that might have embarrassed him, she didn't feel all that bad.

She made her way toward Coach K, who was standing at the sideline with one of the assistants—was it Coach D'Annolfo?

"So, Sackett," Coach K said, and whipped off his sunglasses to wipe a hand across his brow. He stared down at his clipboard without meeting her eye. Coach D seemed especially interested in the cord attached to his whistle.

"Am I getting cut?" asked Ava. Her voice came out in a croaky whisper.

"What?" Now he looked straight at her. "No. Well, maybe, but I don't know yet." He sighed with apparent exasperation and began again.

Ava waited, holding her breath.

"It's not so simple," said Coach K, sounding a tiny bit less gruff than before. "Tomorrow we wear pads, and I'm concerned about the contact. Like I said, I need to bring this matter up with the athletic director."

Coach D nodded in agreement but said nothing.

"But there's nothing in the rules. I checked," said Ava.

"Yes, yes, I know that. But there may be some liability issues involved, and I need to get the go-ahead. I'll try to have it resolved by practice time tomorrow."

Ava nodded, feeling a big lump in her throat. She turned to head toward the locker room.

"Sackett!"

She turned back.

"You looked good out there," said Coach K.

Coach D nodded.

"Second-fastest time in the pro-agility test," Coach K said. "Good work."

She turned around quickly so they couldn't see how big her smile got, and walked away with a little more bounce in her step.

Ava barely made the late bus home. As they drove, she kept smiling to herself, thinking about what Coach K had said. She considered texting Charlie, her sort-of boyfriend back home. He'd understand about the pro-agility test. He played football too. But she decided not to. They hadn't really been texting much recently.

She shouted hello to her mom in the kitchen and ran up the front stairs to shower. She could smell the chili cooking and realized she was starving.

A few minutes later she joined the rest of her family at the dinner table, her hair still dripping. Alex was talking a mile a minute about how she'd gotten her hundred signatures and what was going to happen in the next phase of her campaign, and how glad she was to have gotten ahead with her studying over the weekend because she had a million, no, a zillion posters to finish tonight.

"And what's doubly lucky is, our science class is going on a field trip to the science museum tomorrow," Alex said, "so I don't have any homework for tonight. Can I get a ride with you and Tommy tomorrow morning, Daddy? I need to get to school early to put up my posters before we leave for the museum."

"Sure, thing, Al," said Coach. Then he turned to Ava. "So how'd it go at tryouts today, sport?"

"Good and bad," Ava replied. She stirred her bowl of chili slowly.

Mrs. Sackett set down her glass and looked carefully at Ava. "Honey? Did you make the team?"

"Tryouts are going to be most of the week," said Ava. "Today was just testing and conditioning, and I think I did okay. But Coach K said I might not be allowed to play, because I'm a girl."

Coach pursed his lips.

"Lame," pronounced Tommy as he helped himself to seconds on chili.

"I was worried that might happen," said Alex, sighing.

Mrs. Sackett's eyes blazed. "What is he talking about?" she said, indignation written across her face. "Of course you're allowed! Doesn't Title Nine mean anything to anyone around here?"

"What's Title Nine?" asked Alex.

Mrs. Sackett looked at her, took a deep breath,

and replied, "It was a law passed way back in the early 1970s that said there can be no discrimination based on a person's gender. In other words, girls get to play the same sports boys do, and if there's not an equivalent girls' team, a girl should be allowed to play with the boys."

"Oh!" said Alex. "Then there should be no problem!"

"Coach K says there might be a problem," said Ava. She told them what he had said about bringing it up with the athletic director.

"If they tell you anything other than you're allowed to play, your father and I will be there first thing tomorrow to meet with them," said Mrs. Sackett. She turned to Coach. "Right?"

Coach had remained quiet during the conversation. He set down his fork and cleared his throat. "Not so fast, Laura," he said.

Mrs. Sackett raised her eyebrows.

"You know as well as I do that coaches don't welcome parents who fight their kids' battles," he said.

"But this is—"

Coach raised a hand so he could continue. "This is Ava's situation," he finished. "She needs to work things out as best she can."

"But Michael, if this escalates into a big deal with the district, she's going to need us."

"If that happens, we'll be there to support her," he agreed. "But for now we need to let Ava handle it on her own. It should stay between her and her coach."

"But—"

"Mom," said Ava, "Coach is right. I'll wait and see what Coach K says tomorrow. I've done my homework—well, not my actual homework, but I've researched the rules and stuff. I want to make the team because I'm good enough, not because I'm a girl or because my parents made a big fuss, or worst of all, because I'm Coach Sackett's daughter."

"You go, Ave," said Tommy approvingly.

"What was the matter with volleyball, again?" asked Alex.

Ava glared at her. Tommy threw a piece of roll at Alex.

"All right, never mind," said Alex with a shrug.

"So we'll wait and see," said Coach.

"Okay, can we get back to me for a minute?" asked Alex.

The rest of the family groaned.

"Mom, I really need an outfit for my first

campaign speech," said Alex, undaunted. "It's this Friday at lunchtime, although there's a final speech next week. For this one, all three of us have to speak for three minutes, and then the students have a few minutes to ask us questions. I think I should wear a snappy red blazer—isn't that what candidates wear on television?"

"Are you going to be on television?" asked Tommy.

Alex rolled her eyes. "That's not the point."

"Honey, we've spent enough money on clothes for you this year," said Mrs. Sackett.

"She can have some of whatever you would have spent on me," said Ava with a shrug.

"No, she can't," said Mrs. Sackett firmly. "But I have been planning a trip to a thrift store I heard about around here. I'm hoping I can find some costume jewelry for my new ceramics project. You can come along with me if you want. Maybe you can find something there that you can afford with your allowance money."

"Good idea!" said Alex, jumping up from the table. She cleared away her plate and tried to take Tommy's, but he shook his head and pointed at the pot of chili, indicating that he wanted a third helping.

"I'll be upstairs, working on my posters," said Alex. "I need to come up with a good campaign slogan."

"I've got one," said Tommy. "'Vote for Alex. Because Otherwise Her Family Will Go Bonkers.'"

"Ha-ha," said Alex, and left the kitchen.

CHAPTER FIVE

"Gah!" yelled Alex out loud. She was in her room, sitting on the floor with a fan of poster boards around her, her laptop on her lap.

Ava was just passing by her room and poked her head in. "Was that you who just yelled?"

"Yes!" Alex said hotly. "Sorry," she added, more calmly. "I didn't mean to startle you. But it's been really frustrating trying to come up with a decent slogan. Nothing rhymes with 'Alex.' Not a thing!"

Ava suppressed a grin and came in and sat down on Alex's bed. "Need some help brainstorming?"

Alex scowled. "I doubt you can help," she

said. "Why couldn't they have named me Ann or Pat, or even Sandy?"

"How about 'Sackett'?" suggested Ava. "'Sackett to me'?"

Alex gave her a look.

"Yeah, no," said Ava after some consideration. "How about, 'Sackett can hack it!'?"

Alex blew out a frustrated breath. "No, thanks," she said.

"I have one!" said Ava, bouncing up and down on the bed excitedly. "How about 'Count on Someone Who Counts!'? See? Kind of a play on words—they can depend on you, plus everyone knows you're really good at math."

"Yeah, great, so I'd get all of three votes. From the math club," said Alex dryly. "And probably not even those—I'm sure Ella's got the whole math and science clubs voting for her."

"Well, I know Corey's going to vote for you," said Ava. "He told me at tryouts today."

That got Alex's attention. She closed her computer. "How did it come up?" she asked Ava eagerly.

Ava shrugged. "He just said it as we were stretching after practice was over," she said.

Alex felt herself flushing. Good thing it

was just in front of Ava. She'd vowed to treat Corey like any other seventh-grade guy. But she couldn't stop her heartbeat from quickening when she thought about him. She needed to get more control over this situation. She didn't want anyone to think she still had a crush on him.

Ava must not have noticed her sister blushing, because she'd moved on in the conversation. "But both Logan and Xander are also on the team," she said. "And Logan was going on and on about how he's definitely got the jock vote."

Alex's eyes flashed. "I can't believe how arrogant that guy is!" she said. "Did it ever occur to him that a few jocks might vote for me because of my last name? I mean, being Coach Sackett's daughter has got to count for something."

"Maybe," said Ava. "And also, his friend Xander is a kicker like me. It looks like we're both competing for the same position. So that should be fun."

Alex considered this new information. It was definitely not a good thing that her twin sister was competing for a position with Logan Medina's best friend. "Wow, Ave," she said. "I didn't really think about how much this football tryout of yours might adversely affect my campaign."

Ava stood up. Her lips were pressed together into a tight line, and her chin was all crumpled up.

Alex felt alarmed. Why was Ava so upset? What had she said that was so bad?

"Ave? What's wrong?" asked Alex.

Ava didn't answer. She shook her head quickly and moved toward the door.

"I was just saying things are really complicated," said Alex. "I mean, they're already complicated, with you being Daddy's daughter and all, and everyone in my homeroom knows that Mr. Kenerson is, like, a fanatic about Daddy's team. There's no way you trying out isn't going to be complicated, since your dad is the high school coach. I was just saying—"

"I heard what you were saying," said Ava, her voice full of hurt. "You're worried that what I do is going to affect your precious campaign. Well, it's pretty mean of you to bring up the fact that Coach Kenerson might keep me on the roster just because my last name is Sackett."

"I was only—"

"Especially after you just finished saying you

might have a chance to get jock votes because you're the daughter of the high school football coach. Talk about double standards! What makes it okay that you want to use your last name to get yourself elected?"

And before Alex could answer, Ava left the room, shutting the door behind her with force.

CHAPTER SIX

Tuesday morning Alex sat in the backseat of Coach's car clutching her stack of posters, half listening to Coach and Tommy in the front seat, talking about Friday night's upcoming game against the Spartans. As usual, she was quick to tune out the conversation, which was heavy with football jargon and offensive patterns and defensive strategies. For the millionth time, she thought about how complex football was.

She reflected on the sort-of fight she'd had with Ava last night. She was still not sure why Ava had gotten so upset with her. She wished the football tryouts and the election didn't have to happen at the exact same time. It made everything so much more convoluted. Well, maybe it would resolve itself, if Coach Kenerson told Ava she couldn't play. That would certainly make Alex's life easier. As soon as she'd thought it, she felt guilty.

They pulled up in front of the middle school. It was weird to be here this early, before the buses that clogged up the semicircular drive, before swarms of chattering middle schoolers had arrived. The parking lot was about half-full of cars, and Alex saw two teachers, a man and a woman whom she didn't recognize, trudging in, both laden down with heavy-looking briefcases and large, steaming cups of coffee. Teachers drank a lot of coffee, it seemed.

Alex said good-bye to her father and Tommy and went inside. She checked in with Mrs. Gusman at the front office, who gave her the approved wall-mounting double-stick tape that the custodians had said wouldn't mark the walls. Then she set about putting up her posters in the seventh-grade wing, near the auditorium, the locker room areas, and finally, outside the cafeteria.

It didn't take that long. She'd only made eight posters, and those had taken hours. Hers seemed to be the first ones up—she didn't see any of Logan's or Ella's. That would likely be a temporary situation. No doubt their posters would be plastered all over the school soon enough.

As she finished mounting the last one outside the cafeteria, she stepped back to survey it. *Not bad,* she thought. She hadn't come up with anything clever for a campaign slogan, so she'd finally decided on something straightforward: VOTE FOR ALEX SACKETT! SEVENTH-GRADE CLASS PRESIDENT. She'd decorated her name with glitter glue, and it looked pretty nice. Below the slogan was a picture of her, a blown-up scan of her school picture from last year. It was an okay picture—she was looking off to one side, smiling widely, and she thought she looked pretty confident and presidential.

By now kids were starting to arrive, probably not yet the kids who took the bus, but those who'd been dropped off by their parents. She discovered she had glitter all over her hands and headed toward the girls' bathroom just outside the cafeteria. That was all she needed—glitter on her clothes and in her hair all day.

She assumed the bathroom would be empty at this early hour, but as she pushed open the swinging door, she realized that it wasn't. A girl was standing near the sinks, an open lunch bag unzipped across the metal ledge below the mirrors.

"Oh! Hey, Lindsey!" Alex said cheerfully. "I didn't expect to see you in here so early!"

Lindsey Davis turned toward Alex. She seemed as surprised to see Alex as Alex was to see her.

"Hey, Alex," she replied curtly, and went back to what she was doing, although Alex wasn't sure exactly what that was.

Alex moved to the sink one away from where Lindsey was standing and washed her hands. She really did have glitter in her hair, she realized ruefully, and after carefully drying her hands, began fishing the glittery specks from her curls. "Glitter from my posters," she said to Lindsey, just in case the other girl might think she was fishing out something much grosser, like dandruff or, even worse, lice.

Lindsey didn't answer, but she seemed eager to finish what she was doing. Alex realized Lindsey was transferring lunch food from a white paper bag to a zip-up green lunch bag with a shoulder strap.

"Oh, right, I forgot Mr. Lehner is taking both his seventh-grade science classes to the museum!" said Alex. When Lindsey didn't respond, she kept up the chatter to fill the uncomfortable silence. "So that means you and Emily are coming too! That's awesome. I've got Madison Jackson for my partner, and she's nice and everything, but I don't know her that well, so I'm so glad you guys will also be there. Plus, Ella Sanchez is in my class, which is awkward because we're both running for class president, so we don't really have a lot to say to each other. Hey! Is that a school lunch? I didn't know they gave those out! Are they an improvement over their hot food?" When Lindsey still didn't immediately answer, Alex kept babbling, even though she knew she was babbling. Lindsey had that effect on her. "Probably the school bag lunch is better, I'm guessing, because it's hard to mess up a sandwich and chips, ha-ha."

"It's fine," snapped Lindsey, who had finished what she was doing. She slung the lunch bag onto her shoulder and dumped the remains of the white paper bag and its contents into the garbage can.

"Yeah, I guess it beats the meat loaf surprise

they're probably serving today," said Alex with a laugh. "I didn't even know the school made bagged lunches for kids going on field trips. I'll remind my dad for the next time. He'll be happy not to have to make my lunch."

Lindsey muttered a quick "See you later" and hurried out of the bathroom.

Alex felt that familiar uneasy feeling up and down her spine. She had upset Lindsey. Again. Somehow. What was it about that girl, and why was it that practically every conversation they had, Alex felt like she'd offended her without having a clue how?

With a heavy sigh, Alex shouldered her own lunch bag and followed Lindsey to where everyone was gathering for the field trip.

Mr. Lehner was standing next to the bus, checking kids off his list as they boarded. They were supposed to sit with their designated partners. Alex and Madison found each other and got in line to board the bus.

Alex caught a glimpse of Emily and Lindsey—partners, of course—who weren't in line yet. Both girls had similar lunch bags slung on their shoulders. Alex felt a pang of what wasn't quite jealousy but rather was that familiar feeling of being left out, which she knew was dumb because Lindsey and Emily had been friends since preschool. As Madison was chattering away next to her, Alex realized she was standing behind the Fowler twins, Tim and Greg. Both boys were in the other science class, so she didn't know them, but she knew of them. Alex had counted four sets of twins at Ashland Middle School, which was a lot, but then again it was a really big school. The Fowlers were identical, just as she and Ava were. She knew from Emily that the Fowler family had seven kids. Alex was pretty sure they weren't very well off. Emily said their dad was in the military and had been on active duty for a while, and their mom worked part-time at the supermarket.

As she lined up behind the Fowlers, she noticed the two of them were carrying their lunches in white paper lunch bags. That was when it struck her like a thunderbolt.

The kids with white bags got reduced-price lunches from the school. Usually no one knew which kids got the reduced-price lunches, because everyone just handed their cards to the lunch lady to swipe. But on field trip days, it was painfully obvious, because the reduced-price lunch kids were supposed to pick up their lunches in the cafeteria first thing in the morning.

So Lindsey was receiving a reduced-price lunch. That was what she'd been doing in the bathroom: transferring her school-issued lunch into her own lunch bag, so people wouldn't know.

Alex felt like kicking herself as she filed onto the bus. No wonder Lindsey had been so short with her. *Why, why,* she thought, *am I always so clueless? Lindsey was embarrassed that I saw her with a reduced-price lunch.* Alex racked her brain, trying to remember what she'd said. Something about how the bag lunch had to be an improvement over hot lunches. But now, as she thought about it, she realized Lindsey always got the school's hot lunch. Should she apologize to Lindsey, or would that make an awkward situation even worse?

When she'd first moved to Ashland, Alex had been on Lindsey's bad side because she'd quickly developed a crush on Corey . . . and it seemed like Corey liked her, too. But once Alex found out that Lindsey liked Corey, she began pretending she had a boyfriend back in Boston named Charlie—she had panicked and named Ava's crush as her own boyfriend—and ever since then Lindsey had been much nicer to her. Except when Alex did things like this.

She wished Ava were here to help her negotiate all this. But Ava was mad at her too.

She groaned softly.

Madison had been chatting away about upcoming cheerleading tryouts, but she broke off midsentence and looked at Alex. "You okay?" she asked her.

Alex nodded. "Yes, fine," she said, trying to muster some enthusiasm. "I just ate too much breakfast this morning, and I have a little stomachache. It'll pass."

Alex didn't see much of Lindsey and Emily at the museum. Mr. Lehner's two sections naturally formed separate groups, and Lindsey and Emily were in the other class. In the morning, both sections had a tour guide for the first hour, but then they had split up with their partners to complete a set of questions based on certain exhibits around the museum. They hadn't even sat together at lunch—the classes had sat separately.

On the bus ride back to school, Alex got a text from her mom.

> Just got out of a
> meeting. I'm at your
> school right now. Happy
> to take you with me to
> that thrift store.

Alex texted her back and told her sure.

CHAPTER SEVEN

On Tuesday after school, Ava stared at herself in the grimy locker-room mirror. She barely recognized the person in the Tiger Cubs practice uniform peering out with anxious eyes from the shiny blue Cubs helmet. It had been awhile since she'd worn a helmet, and she'd forgotten how heavy they were, and how hot her head felt with one on. She was already sweating! But having the uniform and helmet on also felt great. This helmet was fancier than the battered old thing she'd worn last year, back in Massachusetts—it had some sort of gel padding that was supposed to mold to your head.

Coach Kenerson had sought her out at lunch

and told her it was okay to suit up—for today, anyway. The athletic director had told him to tell her this, but said he might have to take it up with the school board. Great.

Her pads were a little too big for her shoulders and shifted a bit. She'd signed up for the right pads for her height and weight, she was sure, but her shoulders were probably narrower than an average boy of her size. Whatever. They'd have to do.

It wasn't like she was the smallest kid trying out by any means. There were at least half a dozen sixth graders who were smaller than she was. *And they'll probably get cut,* a little voice told her. *Or if they do make the squad, they'll never play in a game.* She ignored the little voice and headed outside to the field.

The two captains were already assembling the team for the warm-up laps. She joined the clump of kids toward the back, resolving to keep a wary eye on Andy and Xander. It was a lot different from the day before, running with a helmet and pads. But she knew she'd get used to it, the way she had last year on her Massachusetts team.

No one tried to trip her, which was good. But

she observed Xander and Andy running ahead, side by side, talking nonstop to each other. About her, she was pretty sure.

Then came warm-ups and dynamic stretching. Ava took her place in the back line with the sixth graders. There was no point in making a big deal about the injustice of where to stretch out. She'd need to prove herself to the coaches, not worry about team politics.

Warm-ups went fine, although Ava was keenly aware of the strange energy of the team. There wasn't the typical joking around, chatting, laughing you might ordinarily expect. She was sure it was because of her presence. Why was this such a big deal? It was just football. She remembered something Coach had once said to her several years back, after she'd missed the front end of a one-and-one free throw that could have tied the basketball game. "Ave," he'd said, "sports matter a lot in life, but they also don't matter at all." She hadn't understood what he meant at the time, but now she was beginning to.

After warm-ups, Coach K and the assistants told them to break down into groups according to positions. "Linemen with Coach MacDonald!" he bellowed. "Running backs with Coach

D'Annolfo! Quarterbacks and receivers with me!"

Ava gulped. Where should she go if she was just a kicker? Everyone else seemed to know where to go. Even Xander, whom she'd assumed was also "just" a kicker, had joined the group of linemen. Well, that made sense. He was big, and he looked like he liked to knock people down. Soon she was the only one who hadn't moved toward one of the coaches.

"Sackett!" Coach K growled. "You'll be with us."

Without a word, Ava trotted over to the quarterbacks and receivers. Corey gave her a little twitch of a smile. She recognized Owen Rooney, a kid from her math class, and was troubled to see that Andy Baker had also joined the group. At least Owen seemed nicer than Andy—Ava suspected that her friend Kylie had a crush on him.

They spent the next hour practicing footwork, pass routes, and downfield blocking. It was a lot to absorb, but Ava knew she was pretty good at remembering stuff as long as she could physically practice it. That was why she remembered sports plays more easily than science facts.

At last, toward the final half hour of practice, Coach K announced that anyone interested in kicking should report to Coach MacDonald over at the other end of the field. Ava trotted toward him, and soon there was a small group of kickers. Besides her and Xander, there were three other kids. Ava guessed they were all either sixth or seventh graders.

"We're going to practice kicking from a tee today," said Coach MacDonald, eyeing the five kids in front of him. "That's how a kickoff kicker does it. I realize some of you may turn out to be punters or field goal kickers, but for now, I'm looking for accuracy and consistency, and I don't want to introduce a snap at this point."

All five of them nodded. Ava's heart was pounding. This was just what Coach had said too. That it's fine if you can kick a ball forty yards once, but coaches are looking for players who can kick twenty-five yards consistently.

Coach MacDonald demonstrated the kicking technique. He showed them how to run in on the ball from an angle—from the left side for right-footed kickers, and from the right side for left-footed kickers. Then he asked them to line up according to which foot they kicked with.

Ava remained in the center, uncertain what to do.

"What's the matter, Sackett?" barked Coach MacDonald.

Ava hesitated. "I—I kick from both sides," she said. She saw Xander roll his eyes.

"Choose a side," Coach said gruffly.

Ava got behind a sixth grader, the only other kid who was kicking with his left foot.

Coach MacDonald showed them how to approach the ball, to swing the kicking foot back, to keep the toe down, and to kick it "on the hammer of your metatarsals."

They lined up. Xander went first.

It was a nice kick. Probably about twenty-two yards, Ava estimated.

Then the three younger boys went, one at a time. Two kicked it out of bounds. The lefty ahead of Ava sent the ball skittering and bouncing along the ground, where it came to rest about fifteen yards in front of him.

"I can see we have some technique to learn," said Coach MacDonald. "Sackett. You're next."

It had not escaped Ava's notice that hers was the one name all the coaches seemed to know among the new players.

Probably not a coincidence, she thought.

Ava lined up behind the ball. Was she imagining it, or had all the other players stopped to watch her? The linemen at the other end of the field had been ramming into the sled they used to practice blocking, but from what she could see out of the corner of her eye, they'd paused. Were they pausing to watch her kick? She tried her best to ignore everyone around her, took several steps, and sent the ball flying.

It was a pretty good kick, but it was hard to see where it was going with the sun shining in her eyes. It seemed to be soaring straight, traveling end over end and rotating backward the way it should, but then, as though it were a kite being tugged on a string, it began to curve left. It hit the ground just out of bounds. Great. She heard Coach MacDonald grunt. Was it a disappointed grunt? What other kind would it be? She felt her ears burn and her face get hot, and was glad it was all hidden beneath her helmet. She'd let the pressure get to her. She needed to concentrate and forget about all the eyes on her. What would she do in a game situation if she let this affect her?

They each had two more chances, and this

time they each kicked twice in a row. Xander sent both of his kicks flying, and both landed more or less in the exact same spot, about twenty-two yards away.

Coach MacDonald grunted again, and Ava decided this was a grunt of approval. Consistency. That was what the coaches wanted. She watched him make a note on his clipboard.

The other three kids managed to kick the ball in the air without it going out of bounds at least once each, although nowhere near as far as Xander had.

For Ava's second kick, she gained some lift but didn't feel she'd hit it in the "sweet spot." Sure enough, the ball went about twenty yards. Okay, but not great. She knew she could kick it farther than that. She'd done so a zillion times with Tommy snapping the ball for her.

For her last kick, Ava closed her eyes and heaved a calming breath. She needed to do some brief mental preparation. This time she wouldn't be nervous. What good was a kicker who got nervous? By definition, a kicker was supposed to thrive on pressure, to want to perform under the most stressful possible conditions, to ignore the shouts and jeers of the opposing fans. She imagined this was the final minute of a tied game. Everything depended on her.

She opened her eyes, took a running step, and launched the ball.

She knew it was a good kick the second it left her shoe. She'd hit it from just the right part of her foot, like a soccer ball. It sailed high, traveling end over end through the air, silhouetted against the sky. The other kickers and Coach MacDonald all shielded their eyes against the bright sun to see where it landed.

It looked like about a forty-two-yard kick. Ava resisted a strong urge to pump the air with her fist. Instead she looked calmly at Coach MacDonald. He grunted and made a note on his clipboard.

CHAPTER EIGHT

"So what meeting did you have around here?" Alex asked her mom as she buckled her seat belt.

Her mom pulled away from the front of the school and didn't answer right away. Then she said, "I had a meeting about Ava."

Alex turned to look at her in surprise. "About her ADHD? I thought she was doing okay with that."

"She is. Or anyway, we're working on getting her a tutor. It wasn't about that. It was about football."

"Oh," said Alex. "What's going on with that? I didn't see her at lunch today because of our field trip."

"To be honest, Alex, Ava doesn't know that I met with Coach Kenerson. And neither does your father, for that matter. But Mr. Kenerson was very nice about agreeing to it. I just wanted to find out where he stands on the tryout issue. I wanted to know what he personally thinks. It turns out that he's fine with Ava playing, but it seems there are others who are objecting. Other parents."

"Let me guess. The Kellys?"

Mrs. Sackett didn't say yes or no, but Alex could tell by the look on her face that she'd guessed correctly. The Kellys were the parents of a player on the high school team, the star quarterback, PJ. And they'd been giving her dad a hard time from day one of his taking over as coach of the team.

Alex sighed. This day was not the best kickoff to her presidential campaign. First there was the whole scene with Lindsey in the girls' bathroom this morning. Lindsey had barely spoken to her after that, even during the rare moments of the field trip where the classes had mixed and Alex and Emily had been chatting away. And now Ava playing football was starting to look like a real issue. "So what's going to happen now?"

Mrs. Sackett slowed to a stop to allow a

crossing guard to help a group of elementary school kids. The guard waved the okay, and they started up again. "I'm not sure," she said. "But it may go to the school board. This may become a much bigger issue than just a discussion between Ava and her coach."

"Terrific," said Alex. "Why couldn't I have been born with a twin sister who does normal sports, like soccer or cheerleading?"

"I don't want to hear that, Alexandra," said Mrs. Sackett sternly. "Your job is to support your sister, not criticize her."

"I meant the question rhetorically," said Alex. "Of course I support her."

"Good," Mrs. Sackett said as she slowed the car down. "I think this is the place. And that car just pulled out. We can park right in front!"

Alex scrutinized the storefront as her mom pulled up alongside a parked car and then carefully backed into the empty space behind it.

"Carolee's Consignment, huh? This doesn't look like the thrift stores we used to go to in Boston," she said dubiously.

"Keep an open mind," said her mother, turning off the engine. "That's the fun of these places. You never know what you might come across. Maybe you'll find that snappy red blazer you want."

"Maybe," said Alex. "It's worth a look."

A little bell dinged as Alex pushed open the heavy door, holding it for her mom. She was met with the familiar thrift-store smell: a combination of old leather, old-fashioned cologne, and dust. She loved that smell.

Still, at first glance, this was not the same kind of store they had gone to back in Boston. Whereas those had been frequented by hipster twentysomethings and fashion-forward girls like her on the prowl for retro cool, this store seemed more like a store for people who were really in search of a bargain.

Along one wall were three racks of clothes labeled $5/$10/TWO ITEMS FOR $15. There were lots of children's clothes in one area, and a section of hunting wear in another. *That* you didn't see in Boston. But Alex loved to shop no matter what, so she looked around and decided to start in the jewelry section.

"Oh, good, I see some old glassware," said her mom, moving toward the back of the store.

Alex checked out a case full of old necklaces. It was mildly disappointing; mostly old-lady-looking stuff.

A girl emerged from one of the dressing rooms at the rear of the store. Her back was to Alex, but Alex thought she recognized the girl's long, shiny ponytail.

"Mom, this dress smells funny," the girl said to her mother, who was sitting in an old, thread-bare armchair, thumbing through a magazine. "Plus, it's way too long on me."

"We can hem it," said her mom. "Turn around and let me see the back."

The girl gave an exasperated sigh and turned around. As she did so, her eyes met Alex's.

It was Lindsey.

Alex waved at her. "Hey, Lindsey!" she called across the store.

Lindsey weakly waggled three of her fingers at Alex and dove back into the dressing room.

Alex stood, unsure what to do. Should she keep pretending to be engrossed in the jewelry case, or should she hurry back to the dressing room area to wait for Lindsey to emerge? She wanted to make things up to Lindsey after her cluelessness in the bathroom this morning, but she didn't want to come across as too eager. She decided to keep studying the jewelry.

Lindsey must have changed in lightning-fast

time, because she emerged fully dressed just a minute later, carrying the dress she'd been trying on. After a hasty, whispered conversation with her mother, Lindsey finally thrust the dress into Mrs. Davis's hands. Her mom made her way toward the register at the front of the store, but Lindsey didn't make an effort to move in Alex's direction. Instead she stood in the dressing room area and flipped listlessly through a rack of ugly belts.

Alex decided to make the first move, promising herself she wouldn't say anything to offend Lindsey.

"So do you come to this store often?" she asked Lindsey as she joined her next to the belt rack. "This is my first time, but I love thrift shops. My friends and I used to go to them all the time back in Boston. And my mom is always looking for old glass or jewelry and stuff for her pottery."

Lindsey said nothing, so to fill the awkward pause, Alex prattled on in her false-cheerful voice. "I came to find a red blazer for my speech this Friday, but I don't think they have one here. Did you find anything good?"

"I think my mom is ready to go," mumbled Lindsey. "I'll see you tomorrow at school."

And a second later, she had dragged her mom out of the store.

Alex stared after her, contemplating Lindsey's behavior. She'd seemed more embarrassed than anything else. Why would she be embarrassed? What was the big deal about running into someone at a thrift store?

This time it dawned on her more quickly.

She's shopping here because she can't afford to shop at other stores, not because she thinks it's cool.

No wonder Lindsey had seemed so embarrassed. Twice in one day, Alex had inadvertently shown up at just the wrong place at the wrong time. First she had seen Lindsey transfer her school-issued lunch into her own bag. And then she had seen her shopping at a thrift store. *Lindsey's family must really be hurting for money,* Alex thought, *and I'm the one kid from school who has witnessed firsthand what she's going through.*

"Did you find your red blazer?" asked her mom. Mrs. Sackett was carrying several thick glass bottles, the sort they probably used for medicine back in the olden days.

"No, but that's okay," said Alex, still thinking of Lindsey. "I'll make do with something from my closet."

CHAPTER NINE

Ava was completely winded. She took off her helmet and gulped fresh air. Must be the pads. They'd take some getting used to, especially in this unfamiliar Texas climate.

Her second-ever Ashland practice was over. They hadn't run nearly as much as they had yesterday, but it had still been tough.

"Sackett! A word."

She trotted over to Coach K, who was standing on the sideline, out of earshot of the locker room area.

"Heard you did a nice job kicking today, Sackett," he said.

"Thanks," she replied, and waited.

"So here's the deal. Good news, bad news. You've made the team. But you can't play. At least, not just yet."

A lump immediately rose in her throat, and she felt her eyes mist up with hot tears, but she kept quiet and waited to hear what he would say next.

"It seems that while there's nothing in the rule book saying girls aren't allowed to play, there's a clause in the district bylaws that says the school board may prevent a child from playing if it has any concerns about the child's safety, or the safety of others. There are some parents who have called the athletic director. They want it brought up before the school board at the next meeting."

"Was it the Kellys?" asked Ava.

Coach K took off his sunglasses and began polishing them furiously on his pant leg.

So it was the Kellys, Ava thought. "Why do they care?" she asked.

Coach put his glasses back on and coughed. He looked like he wanted to say something but thought better of it. Then he sighed and looked at her. "Andy Baker."

"What about him?"

"He's Doug Kelly's nephew. That's why they care."

"Oh," said Ava. That explained why the Kellys were so interested in the middle school football team. "When is the next meeting?" she asked in a tiny voice.

"Next Wednesday. A week from tomorrow."

"But . . . that's three days before the first game!"

"I know," he said, nodding grimly. "I'm sorry, Sackett. You're a good kicker, and I could use you. But this is out of my hands. I can give you a playbook to study while you wait for their decision, so you'll at least be familiar with the I formation and the shotgun. I'm sure you'll pick it up quickly."

He turned and strode away from her. She swallowed down the lump in her throat and headed toward the girls' locker room. Several guys from the team were talking in low voices in small groups outside the boys' locker room door, but no one said anything to her as she walked past, not looking up.

Just before she headed in, her eye caught some movement through the window that led to the athletic offices. Coach Kenerson was in with the athletic director. And sitting just opposite the desk were a man and a woman. The Kellys.

Dinner that night was a somber affair. Somehow Ava's mom and dad already knew about what Coach K had said to her.

For a few minutes, there was just the clinking of silverware.

Coach set down his fork and cleared his throat, started to say something, then seemed to think better of it and picked up his fork again.

Mrs. Sackett kept looking from Ava to Coach and back again. Ava thought her mom looked like she was bursting to speak, but she was clearly waiting for Coach to broach the subject.

Next to her, Alex was at a rare loss for words. Actually, Ava noticed that when she looked more closely at her twin that Alex's lips were moving. Ava leaned sideways a little, cocking an ear to hear what she was saying. She decided Alex must be practicing the speech she had to give on Friday.

It was Tommy who finally broke the ice.

"Tough day out there, huh, Avesy?"

That seemed to energize their parents, who both spoke at once.

"It's outrageous," said Mrs. Sackett. "Beyond belief that they would—"

"It's not Coach Kenerson's decision," said Coach. "But it's a tough situation—"

They both left off speaking. Tommy spoke up again. "So how'd you actually do in tryouts? Would you be on the team if you were a dude?"

Ava nodded. "Coach K said I technically made the team. I kicked pretty well today, and yesterday during conditioning I had the second-fastest time in the pro-agility test and the fourth-fastest time in the shuttle endurance drill."

Coach looked impressed. "You've got both speed and quickness, honey," he said approvingly.

"Aren't those the same?" Alex asked, pausing midway through practicing her speech.

"Speed is how fast you can go, but quickness is how fast you can change speed or direction," Coach explained.

Alex nodded and tuned them out again.

"And today they made me practice with the quarterbacks and receivers," Ava continued. "Because I guess they didn't know where else to put me."

Mrs. Sackett elbowed Coach meaningfully. "Michael. Tell Ava what we've decided."

Ava pushed away her uneaten spaghetti and looked at her dad. She had no idea what he was going to say. He was so adamant about parents not fighting kids' battles for them, especially when it came to sports. And yet, right now she was feeling pretty unsure what to do.

"Sport," said Coach. "You mother and I are going to support you the best we can with this situation. It's tricky, as I'm sure you know, because I'm the coach of the Tigers."

"But I'm not the coach of the Tigers!" said Mrs. Sackett fiercely. Her eyes were bright, and she had two pink spots on her cheeks. "I can say whatever I want to them!"

"Laur," said Coach, putting a hand over hers. "Ave, we've decided it would be best if your mother came with you next Wednesday to the school board meeting. But in the meantime, you can come to my practices. You can participate in the conditioning we do, and you can practice kicking when we're not using that end of the field."

"And I'll have some time this weekend to work out with you," said Tommy. "I need to do some passing drills and you can be my receiver."

"Thanks," said Ava. "The whole thing just seems so dumb. I don't get why it's such a big deal. I'm not any more likely to get hurt than any of the guys."

"I know, right?" Alex finally piped up.

Ava looked at her.

Alex shrugged. "Just trying to be supportive," she said.

"Thanks a lot," said Ava dryly.

"And I can help you study your playbook," said Mrs. Sackett. "So you'll be able to come back knowing the plays."

"Great," said Ava. "Not exactly the perfect strategy for a kid with ADHD. Studying the playbook makes me go cross-eyed. I learn so much better when I actually do them."

"Speaking of Ava's ADHD," said Tommy cheerfully, "my friend Luke says he wouldn't mind interviewing to be a tutor for her. He wants to be a teacher, I guess."

"Good for him," said Coach. "We'll have to talk to him." He turned toward Alex. "And how's the campaign going, honey?"

"Oh, the campaign itself is fine," said Alex. "But I don't think I have a chance at winning. Logan has the jock vote, and Ella has the brain vote, so that leaves me the artsy kids and the delinquents, and I don't think either of those groups even know there's an election. Plus, Logan and Ella both seem to have unlimited campaign funds. Logan has no end of swag to pass out. His staffers were handing out candy bars yesterday"—she looked accusingly at Ava—"and today it was pencils with 'Vote for Logan' on them. And Ella's posters look like they were done by professionals, which they were, because her dad owns a chain of copy shops."

"Sounds like Ashland Middle School needs some campaign finance reform," said Tommy.

"Go ahead and make a joke," said Alex, "but it's actually so not funny. They're obviously both independently wealthy, and I don't think it's fair."

"Well, now you'll be known as the candidate whose sister wants to play on the football team," said Tommy optimistically.

Ava smiled.

Alex frowned. "I hope that doesn't happen, Tommy," she said. Then she brightened. "Anyway, it's not the sort of thing middle school kids care about. I'm sure no one's going to pay any attention to what's going on with Ava and the school board."

CHAPTER TEN

But as they got off the bus the next day, Alex quickly realized that Ava seemed to be all anyone was talking about.

"Good for you, Ava!" yelled a girl.

"Girls can't play football!" yelled a boy.

A group of girls was arguing with a group of boys, and Alex was pretty sure she heard "football" and "Sackett."

Other groups of kids just stopped talking and watched Alex and Ava make their way through the crowd.

"Everyone's staring at us," said Alex through a frozen smile. She was trying to speak without moving her lips, like a ventriloquist.

"Sure looks that way," Ava muttered back, as the two walked up the front steps of the school.

Ms. Farmen, the principal, was standing at the top of the stairs as she did most mornings, greeting kids as they walked in. As Alex and Ava passed her, she flashed Ava an encouraging smile.

"Well, it looks like you've got Ms. Farmen's support, at least," said Alex. "She probably can't be too obvious about it, though, because she's the principal and she answers to the school board." She looked around the lobby at the posters plastered on every wall. Of course there were posters for the sixth- and eighth-grade candidates, and there was the one of hers she'd put up yesterday morning, but it felt as though everywhere she turned she saw Logan and Ella's posters.

A group of eighth-grade girls walked past them. "Way to go, Ava!" said one.

A group of seventh-grade girls Alex vaguely recognized from the one science club meeting she'd attended walked past from the other direction. "Aren't you afraid you're going to get hurt?" asked one of them.

Ava opened her mouth to respond, but Alex poked her in the side. "It's better to ignore them!" she whispered.

"Football's for guys," grunted a boy, and the group he was walking with all nodded.

Mr. Fifer, the music teacher, passed by as they arrived at their lockers. He stopped and gave Ava a double thumbs-up, pausing briefly as though waiting for someone to snap his picture.

"You go, girl!" he said enthusiastically, and walked on.

Ava cringed. "Who even says that anymore besides nerdy teachers and parents?" she asked Alex.

Alex shook her head darkly. "I had no idea this was going to be such a big deal," she said. "It's definitely distracting my voters from the issues at hand. I don't like it one bit."

Ava slammed her locker closed and glared at Alex. "It isn't always all about you, Al," she said. "Do you think I want to be the center of attention? All I want to do is play."

Before Alex could respond, Kylie McClaire appeared on the other side of Ava. "Oh my," she said, grinning. "You do know how to cause a stir, Sackett girls! The whole school is talking about you and the school board meeting next Wednesday!"

"It is?" asked Alex, growing more despondent by the minute.

"Mm-hmm." Kylie nodded, her long, dangly earrings jangling. "And it sounds like Logan Medina is trying to turn it to his advantage, saying stupid stuff about how 'girls should be girls'"—she crooked her fingers in the air as quotes—"and how the Sackett twins are troublemakers, et cetera."

"He said that?" asked Alex weakly.

"Yeah, but I think it's going to hurt him," said Kylie. "He'll lose the girl vote if he keeps this up." She turned to Ava, who had remained quiet during this whole exchange. "You okay?" she asked her.

Ava nodded. "The worst thing is all the whispering I see kids doing. I have no idea if they're for or against. And I guess I don't care. But still—it's awkward."

It was still early, and when Alex arrived at her homeroom classroom she found Emily and Lindsey chatting outside the door. Lindsey was wearing the dress she'd been trying on at the thrift shop. Her mom must have hemmed it, and it looked adorable on her.

"Hey, Alex!" said Emily, cheerful and welcoming as ever. "Don't you love Lindsey's new dress? She got it at Spruce. Isn't it just the prettiest thing you've ever seen?"

"She got it at—wait." Alex wrinkled her brow. She was positive that was the dress . . . oh. Of course. Lindsey didn't want Emily to know she'd been shopping at a thrift store. She'd lied about where she'd gotten her dress. "Spruce!" said Alex hastily, her face lighting up. "Of course! It looks—it looks awesome on you, Lindsey."

The worried furrow on Lindsey's face smoothed and relaxed. She smiled gratefully at Alex, clearly relieved that Alex was playing along. "Thanks," she said. "So how's the campaign going?"

Alex was momentarily shocked that Lindsey was initiating conversation with her. It was the first time in a while—she had been so standoffish lately. "Um, fine!" said Alex. "Well, mostly fine. Logan seems to have an entire staff at his disposal. He's got them passing out candy, helping him with posters, doling out pencils. And Ella has the public relations thing wrapped up. It's amazing how many posters she's got up, and what professional quality they are."

"That's no fair! Hmm . . . what if we help you?" suggested Lindsey.

"Yes! Let's help!" said Emily with genuine enthusiasm.

Again, Alex was startled by Lindsey's warmth, and by her offer. Lindsey and Emily had said they would help a while ago, but so far they hadn't been around much, and Alex had assumed they hadn't really meant it.

"Wow, that would be awesome," said Alex.

"Great," said Lindsey. "We all have the same lunch period, right?" When Alex and Emily nodded, Lindsey said, "Let's sign out the art room. We can make a bunch more posters."

The bell rang, and Alex and Lindsey said good-bye to Emily, who headed off to her homeroom class.

"I'll see if other kids want to come help us!" said Lindsey as she slid into her desk. Alex slid into the one next to her, elated but perplexed.

"Wait, Lindsey did that?" Ava almost dropped the book she was holding and stared incredulously at Alex.

"I know. It's crazy, isn't it? She started being nice just after I went along with a lie she told."

Ava's eyes widened. She'd never been a big fan of Lindsey and hadn't understood why her sister wanted so desperately to be accepted by her. Sure, she was part of the "cool" crowd, and belonging was really important to Alex, but it was clear that Lindsey didn't like Alex, and that bothered Ava. Of course, that could be because of the whole Corey issue. But Alex had turned him down, and Lindsey still hadn't been super nice to her. Until now, Ava supposed.

"What do you think made her change her mind about you?" asked Ava.

Alex explained how she had run into Lindsey in the thrift shop, and how she had seen her in the girls' bathroom before the field trip. "So after I saw her in two different embarrassing situations—embarrassing for her, I think, even though I didn't have a clue why they'd be embarrassing—she's been totally nice to me. She rounded up half a dozen kids and they all helped make twelve more posters, and then she even insisted on putting them up during lunch. Why do you think she's doing this?"

Ava stopped putting in her locker combination

and turned to her twin. "Al, it's really obvious."

"It is?" Alex looked relieved.

"She probably feels she owes you now because you know this secret about her. You know that her family is struggling, and she's a proud person, and she doesn't want it to get around. It's like an unspoken deal: If you can be discreet about all this, she'll repay you by help-ing you get elected. Maybe it's not totally that clear in her mind, but I think she feels she has a debt to repay."

Alex still didn't seem to get it. Ava knew how much her sister relied on her to help inter-pret subtle stuff like this, so it was good that they were talking again. Ava had been feeling hurt that Alex wasn't getting behind her about her right to try out for football, but maybe, Ava thought now, it was just one more example of Alex's self-involvement. It wasn't that Alex didn't care, Ava realized. She just got so wrapped up in her own stuff sometimes that she forget to think about other people's stuff.

"That's so weird," Alex said slowly. "What's the big deal about getting a reduced-price lunch or shopping in a thrift store? I mean, don't you remember back in Boston when Mom hadn't gone back to work yet and Daddy wasn't making very much money and we couldn't afford to go on vacation for like, three summers in a row?"

"I don't think it's the same thing," said Ava. "I think Lindsey has an image to protect. Kylie told me that the Davises have always been one of the better-off families. I think she wants to make it seem like nothing's changed, even though it has."

Alex stared down the hallway as she contemplated this. Then she nudged Ava. "Look at Logan," she said under her breath, gesturing with her chin. "He's totally flirting with that group of girls over there."

"Whatever," said Ava, spinning the dial on her locker. "He's—" She stopped as something fell out and landed on the floor.

Alex stooped to retrieve it and handed it to Ava. "What's that?" she asked.

Ava stared down at it. She felt the heat rise in her face. Without a word, she passed it to Alex.

It was a piece of construction paper with two cutout pictures pasted to it. They looked like photos from old magazines. The picture on the left showed a football player in a three-point stance, one hand on the ground. Someone had drawn curlicues around the sides of the helmet with a bow on top—to indicate that the player was a girl. The person had also drawn a circle around the football player, with a slash through it—girls shouldn't play football. The picture on the right showed an old-fashioned cheerleader with her hair in blond pigtails, wearing a wool sweater and a flouncy skirt. She was doing a dumb-looking leap in the air, shaking her pompoms, and she looked like the least athletic person on earth. The person had drawn an arrow pointing to her. As in—this is what girls should be doing.

There was no name, no message, nothing else written on the paper.

Alex looked perplexed. "What does this even mean?"

"It means," said Ava, her voice shaking with rage, "that I shouldn't play football because I'm a girl. I should be a cheerleader instead."

"That's dumb. You don't even like cheerleading."

"It's a message, Al, that girls should stick to cheerleading. It's so stupid, too . . . the whole reason they say they don't want me to play football is so I don't get hurt, but cheerleaders get hurt just as much if not more than football players do. Plus, there are tons of boys who are cheerleaders. Has this person been living under a rock?"

"Just ignore it, Ave," said Alex. "Anyway, I better run. Emily and Lindsey promised to listen to me practice my speech."

Ava watched her sister walk away. She couldn't believe how much Alex had downplayed this. It was a big deal. Someone had gone to a lot of trouble to make this dumb sign and shove it into her locker while she was at lunch. She looked around the hallway at all the chattering, laughing kids at their lockers. One of them had sent her this message. It could have been anyone.

CHAPTER ELEVEN

On Friday, Alex woke up with her stomach turning in somersaults. Today was speech day. It wasn't like she wasn't prepared. She knew her speech by heart. She'd practiced it over and over and over until close to midnight, and she could recite it in her sleep. She probably had said it in her sleep, come to think of it. Still, this was a big moment in her campaign. A speech in front of the whole seventh grade. They were rearranging the lunch blocks, extending them by fifteen minutes for each grade, to give the candidates for president time to make a three-minute speech, followed by a question-and-answer session. Due to time constraints, the other candidates—for vice president, secretary, and treasurer—would be distributing their one-paragraph speeches in written form to everyone in homeroom.

"Well, now, don't you look presidential!" said Tommy as Alex walked into the kitchen half an hour later. She hadn't found a snappy red blazer, but she was wearing the next best thing—a crisp white blouse with a Peter Pan collar and an A-line red skirt.

"Pretty, hon," said Mrs. Sackett, plunking down a plate of scrambled eggs with toast for Alex.

Coach hurried in, fully dressed and tucking in his shirt. "Come on, Tom. We've got to get going. We've got a big day ahead of us."

"Good luck in your game, you two," said Alex as the two of them headed for the door. "Wish we could be there!"

"Thanks, sweetheart," said Coach, giving her a quick kiss on the top of the head as he grabbed his coffee cup off the counter. "Good luck with the speech today." He and Tommy hurried out the door.

"Wait, why can't we go to the game again, Mom?" asked Ava, who had just come clattering down the stairs in—Alex noted with mild disap-proval—a football jersey.

"Because it's almost two hours away," said her mother patiently. "And it would mean pulling you out of school early, which I do not think is a good thing to do for a football game. You can watch it on the computer—it's streaming through the school website. I'll have it all set up for you."

Alex pushed away the eggs she'd barely touched and stood up. "I'm too nervous to eat," she said to her mom. "I'm going upstairs to practice my speech a couple more times. Call me when you're ready to go, Ave."

After lunch, Alex sat up on the platform at one end of the cafeteria, looking out at a sea of faces. It was the old stage, one that was rarely used anymore since the school had added on the auditorium, but today it would come in handy as everyone was already sitting, ready for the show.

"We'll go in alphabetical order," Ms. Farmen had told the three candidates. "Remember— three minutes and then I ring my bell. We have to keep this moving so we don't cut into the next class period."

So Alex was second. She sat in her seat between Logan and Ella, mentally preparing the speech she'd practiced. Neither Logan nor Ella said anything to her, or to each other. *They must be as nervous as I am,* Alex thought. She looked at Logan out of the corner of her eye. Actually, he didn't look a bit nervous. He was making faces at a group of guys sitting at a long table toward the front. The guys were all cracking up, shoving one another sideways, and making faces back at him. *It's so not fair,* Alex thought. She wanted this so badly, and had for so long, and here was Logan, messing around with his friends—he didn't seem to care one bit about being president. Yet he was probably the one who would get elected, just because he was popular.

As Ms. Farmen got kids' attention, tapping the mike and calling for quiet, Alex scanned the crowd. There was Ava, sitting next to Kylie at a table toward the back. Ava gave her a little thumbs-up. Alex allowed the corners of her mouth to twitch upward.

There was thunderous applause and whistles as Ms. Farmen introduced Logan.

He unfolded his long legs, stood up, and ambled to the podium. Alex was grudgingly impressed that he had no notes to refer to. Maybe he had prepared as carefully as she but was better at pretending to be nonchalant.

"Thanks, Ms. Farmen," he said, speaking in that smooth-as-honey voice. "My name is Logan Medina, and I think I would be a great class president. Here's why."

He had a little grin on his face, but Alex could tell he was making this up as he went along. Surely it wasn't possible that he hadn't prepared at all!

"Because," Logan continued, "Ashland Middle is an awesome school and it needs an awesome president!"

There was an eruption of cheers and "Dude!" calls from the table of guys.

"Ashland rules!" he yelled, pumping his fist in the air. The place went wild. Now Logan seemed to be considering what to say next. He glanced over at Alex and Ella.

"My opponents are great and all, but do we really need a president who spends her life in the science lab? What if she accidentally blew up the school or whatever?"

This drew huge amounts of laughter and cheers. Alex felt Ella stiffen beside her.

"Or a president who's from a family of troublemakers and who thinks girls should play guys' sports? Our football team is already going to be awesome. Right, dudes? Guys rule!"

Now there was a mixed response from the audience. Logan's table of course went wild with whoops and cheers, as did a few other groups of guys around the cafeteria. But Alex also heard a distinct booing from all around the room. He had some nerve, bringing her sister into the campaign! What right did he have to insult Ava? And yet—her anger now flared up at Ava. Why couldn't she just stick to normal sports for girls? Was she going to be the reason Alex lost this election?

Ms. Farmen stepped to the podium again and was ringing her bell. Alex wasn't sure whether it was because Logan's allotted three minutes were up (mostly used up by the noise from his friends) or to restore order. The bell worked, and the crowd quieted back down quickly. Alex felt Logan drop casually into the seat beside her. She heard Ms. Farmen introduce her, and stood up on shaky legs. She tottered over to the podium.

She was still seething, mostly at Logan, but a tiny bit at Ava for causing this stress. She had her speech ready. It was all about how organized she was, how prepared she would be to listen to her constituents and take up their grievances to the school administration, how her worthy opponents were great representatives of the athletic kids and the smart kids (respectively), but that she, Alex, was "an everyman," someone who didn't fit neatly into any one category and how hers would be a government "of the people, by the people, for the people." That was to be her big finale. There was no time to change it.

But as she stared at the sea of people, including her sister's expectant face, she thought about chucking out what she'd prepared. *I will stand up for my sister. For girls in general. So what if it makes me lose the election? It's the noble thing to do.*

She cleared her throat.

But then again, she thought, *why should I let Ava playing football wreck my chances to be president? It's not like she's been all that considerate about my feelings!*

Precious seconds had already ticked by. She had to act fast. She made the decision—

—and delivered the speech she'd prepared and memorized.

It was perfectly timed out, and she came in

at just under three minutes. The applause was warm but not full of whoops and enthusiasm the way Logan's had been.

She sat down, still trembling slightly. She barely heard Ella's speech, but from what she could tell it was a pretty good one; it was well written, and Ella sounded polished as she delivered it. It got about the same level of applause as her speech had. Logan was going to win for sure.

Ms. Farmen invited kids to ask questions of the candidates. "We have just about three minutes remaining before the bell," she said, "so please keep your questions brief."

A hand shot up near the right side of the room. Ms. Farmen called on the girl, whom Alex didn't know.

"I have a question for Alex," she said.

Alex froze and felt her mouth go dry. She was totally confident fielding questions about her plans as president, but she had a sneaking feeling this question wasn't going to be about that.

"Do you think your sister should be allowed to play for the football team?"

She was right.

There was an immediate murmuring throughout the cafeteria as Alex got to her feet and accepted the microphone from Ms. Farmen.

"Ah," she said. Her mind was whirring. What should she say? Of course she believed Ava should be allowed to play football, but she didn't want to lose voters by saying so. "Um, I believe that sports should be unrelated to politics . . . and as a candidate I think it's important to remain impartial on this issue . . . while I believe girls can do anything boys can do, I, um, think it's also true that I don't want my sister to get hurt, so, ah . . ." She continued to blather on and on, without really saying anything specific. She was dimly aware that the bell rang, and then everyone was bustling around getting ready to go.

She handed the mike back to Ms. Farmen. Had she really spent the whole Q and A on that one question? How would Ava react to her lame, noncommittal answer? She looked at the place where Ava had been sitting.

The seat was empty.

CHAPTER TWELVE

Ava had left the cafeteria before Alex had even finished her long, convoluted answer to the basic question. She felt hot, angry tears in her eyes, but she wiped them away fiercely. Her sister had let her down. Logan had practically invited Alex to challenge him on the issue, and Alex had wimped out. The least she could have done was say something intelligible in answer to the girl's question, but she already sounded like a politician.

After school she headed for the track over at the high school. With the football and the cross-country teams all away, she had it to herself. She ran sprints, did some agility drills, and practiced some kicking. Then she took the late bus home. She planned to eat an early dinner so she could watch Coach and Tommy's game on the webcast.

Alex was already home and was just pulling a veggie frozen pizza out of the oven when Ava walked in.

"Hi, Ave!" she said cheerfully.

"Hi," muttered Ava.

"I already walked Moxy," said Alex. "Because I figured you'd be getting home late."

"Thanks," said Ava, and moved past her sister to head up to her room.

They didn't say much to each other all night. Ava could hear Alex clanking plates and silverware, but she decided to stay in her room until the start of the game and eat her dinner at half-time.

At kickoff time, the two sisters gathered in Coach's office and sat in side-by-side chairs at his desk, watching the webcast on the big desktop computer. Moxy sprawled out on the couch next to them. Normally Moxy was not allowed on the couch, but she understood that when Mrs. Sackett wasn't home, the girls would have no objection.

It was a lopsided game—the Tigers trounced the Spartans. At halftime, the score was 28–7, and Ava went into the kitchen to eat her pizza. Alex made popcorn. Neither girl brought up Alex's speech.

By the start of the fourth quarter, the Tigers were up 38–10. Alex sat flipping through a magazine, only half watching. Ava remained engrossed in the game. Suddenly she breathed in sharply.

"What?" asked Alex quickly, looking at the screen.

"Tommy's in," said Ava.

Their brother, the second-string quarterback now that his teammate Dion had a stress fracture, was getting a chance to play. Coach probably didn't want to risk PJ getting hurt, and he wanted to give Tommy game experience.

A minute later Ava groaned.

"What? What happened? I didn't see what happened!" said Alex.

"He just fumbled the snap," said Ava.

"Aw, Tommy," said Alex softly.

The Tigers ended up winning 38–17. In addition to the fumble, Tommy completed just one of four passes, and that was just for three yards.

When it was over, Ava clicked off the computer and headed into the kitchen to clean up. With a quiet "I'm going to bed," she went upstairs.

Much later she heard Moxy bark twice, her happy bark, and then she heard Tommy and her parents come in. Her clock told her it was fifteen minutes past midnight. There was low murmuring, the clanking of plates and glasses. Of course Tommy would be eating another big meal before bed. Ava turned toward the wall and fell asleep.

The rest of the weekend passed uneventfully. The mood in the Sackett house was somber. Coach watched film in his office. Mrs. Sackett was still working on finishing a big pottery order for a wedding, so she spent most of the weekend at her studio. Tommy kept to his room, banging away on his keyboard. Alex spent a lot of time in her room, working on her final speech, to be delivered at an all-school assembly on Wednesday. The elections would be held on Thursday.

Ava worked on drills at the park near their house and tried to study the playbook, but as she'd predicted, she found it very hard to concentrate on the diagrams. It was so much easier to go through the motions with the team. Tommy and her friend Jack tried to help her a little, but Jack was a soccer and basketball player and didn't really know the football plays. And part of her wondered what the point was. What if the school board decided at the meeting on Wednesday night that she couldn't play? What difference would it make then if she knew the plays or not?

CHAPTER THIRTEEN

Alex woke up Monday morning feeling unprepared for classes, and she hated that feeling. She knew she'd spent way too much time working on her speech over the weekend. She'd neglected her SAT vocabulary cards yet again—it had been over a week since she'd had time to learn even one new word. But Wednesday was so important. She had to nail this next speech.

Once again, speeches would be limited to only three minutes. This time the sixth- and eighth-grade candidates would talk too, so they had to get through nine speeches in one class period. There wasn't any room for going over the time limit, and Ms. Farmen had warned everyone she would not hesitate to ring her bell when their time was up. There would be no time for Q and A. *Which is probably a good thing,* Alex thought grimly, *considering how badly I flubbed that part last week.* She cringed just thinking about it.

At school Lindsey continued to be oddly kind to Alex. She offered to pass out fliers on election day to kids as they got off the bus.

"That's so nice of you, Lindsey," said Alex cautiously. "But I don't have any fliers. Should I make some, do you think?"

"I can help you," said Lindsey eagerly. "And I was thinking I could organize some cheer-leaders from last year's squad to create a cheer for you. We could do it on Wednesday morning before first period."

"Oh, no, please don't bother," said Alex. She was feeling increasingly guilty about Lindsey helping with her campaign because of this "unspoken deal," as Ava called it.

On Tuesday morning Alex and Ava arrived at their lockers to find Lindsey in the process of decorating Alex's locker.

"Oh, shoot!" she said with a laugh. "I wanted to surprise you before you got here! Oh, well.

Like you wouldn't have guessed it was me."

Alex's locker was papered with a big sign that said SHE'S NUMBER ONE! ALEX FOR PRESIDENT! VOTE SACKETT! Lindsey had stuck several balloons to the top part and was sticking tiny silver and gold stars around the edges.

Ava raised an eyebrow as she regarded Alex's locker, but didn't say anything. She opened her own locker, shoved some books and papers in, took some books and papers out, and headed off to homeroom.

Lindsey was still peeling off little shiny stickers and putting them on Alex's locker, talking the whole time. "Almost done here," she said. "I just want to—"

"Lindsey." Alex said it quietly.

Lindsey stopped and looked at her.

"You don't have to do this," said Alex. "I'm not going to tell anyone."

A look of pretend confusion crossed Lindsey's face. "I don't know what you're talking about!" she said. She stared down at her sheet of star stickers.

"About seeing you in the bathroom. And about the thrift store. It's not a big deal. I'm sure no one would care even if they knew, but I'm not going to say anything to anyone, I promise."

Lindsey sighed, and the look of innocent bewilderment disappeared from her face. She glanced to the right and to the left, as though worried they might be overheard, then leaned in closer to Alex. "Okay, thanks," she said. "I—it's been really rough this year. For my family, I mean—we don't have a lot of money right now. My dad says it's temporary, but he's been trying to turn things around with the restaurant for a while now and it's been . . . hard. I hate school lunch. I hate that I have to get it every day." She stopped talking and took a deep breath.

"What happened with the restaurant?" asked Alex.

Lindsey closed her eyes and leaned against the lockers. "My dad was a banker. A really successful one. But he's always loved to cook, and he always wanted to own a restaurant. So he and my mom invested most of our savings in the place, and Corey's parents became their partners and also invested money into the business. It was really starting to do well." She sighed. "It was doing so well, they opened a second restaurant."

Alex waited. Lindsey had a faraway look in

her eye, as though recalling troubled memories.

"But then this chain restaurant offered to buy both restaurants. Corey's parents sold right away, but my parents refused. So the chain people opened one of their restaurants right across the street from our restaurant on purpose, to drive us out of business. And we can't compete with their prices, even though ours has way better food."

"That's so unfair!" said Alex indignantly.

"I know. I even think they did some really underhanded stuff, like posing as customers and writing bad reviews online, and bribing the zoning guy so we couldn't add a bigger parking area."

"That sounds illegal!"

"It probably is. And that's the other complicated thing. See, Corey's mom is a lawyer. When my dad asked her to help him with the legal aspects of the whole thing, she said she thought he should find someone else, someone who wasn't a former partner. Which was weird because he thought they still were partners. So our parents kind of stopped being friends."

So that explained why there was awkwardness between Corey's and Lindsey's families.

Alex nodded. Lindsey seemed to want to go on.

"Sometimes I'm ashamed that we lost most of our money and are having trouble paying for our house," said Lindsey. "But other times I'm proud of my dad for following his dream, even if it hasn't worked out so well."

"I understand being embarrassed about money," said Alex quietly. "I mean, my family's had times when it's been hard and we haven't been able to do stuff other people are able to do. And you always find people with more money than you have. Like in this dumb campaign. I don't know where Ella and Logan get all their campaign money, but I can't even begin to do what they've done in terms of posters, and handing out candy and stuff."

"I think Ella's parents are way involved in her campaign," said Lindsey. "And I know Logan's kind of spoiled. His parents are divorced, and they give him anything he asks for."

Alex nodded. "That makes sense. But anyway, it's really nice of you to help me, but please don't worry about me saying anything to anyone. I think it's awesome that your dad is following his dream, and that's nothing to be ashamed of. I hope you guys fight that chain and win.

And—" Alex broke off, lost in a new thought.

The first bell rang. "You okay?" asked Lindsey.

Alex snapped out of her reverie. "Yes," she said. "You just helped me realize I really owe someone an apology."

"I did?"

Alex nodded vigorously. "You did. I've been awful. But I think I have a way to make up for it. So, thanks!"

Lindsey shrugged. "You're welcome."

CHAPTER FOURTEEN

On Wednesday, Alex once again sat between Logan and Ella, this time on the auditorium stage. The entire school was assembled before her, a sea of faces, and right now everyone was listening to the third of the three sixth-grade candidates, a girl named Chloe Klein, deliver her presidential election speech. The houselights weren't completely down, so Alex could see people's faces. Lindsey, Emily, and Rosa were front row center. A few rows behind them, Ava was sitting next to Kylie. And toward the back were Jack, Corey, and a bunch of guys from the football team. Xander was at the end of that row, sitting next to Andy, and from the dim glow illuminating their faces from time to time, Alex knew they were playing a game on a phone. Which was way against the rules.

Chloe finished her speech just as Ms. Farmen was reaching for the bell. Ms. Farmen wasn't kidding about timing speeches exactly. Everyone politely applauded.

"And next we have the seventh-grade candidates," said Ms. Farmen. "First up will be Logan Medina."

A sizable number of boys in the audience whooped and cheered and yelled "Meh-DEEEEEE-nah!" as Logan ambled to the stage. Alex was amazed at how relaxed he seemed. *Maybe he really should pursue a career in broadcasting or something,* she thought enviously.

Again, Logan had no notes with him. He leaned an elbow nonchalantly on the podium and addressed the audience slightly from the side, as though he were telling them all a confidential bit of news. "Hey, y'all," he said in his low, caramel-smooth voice.

More applause, whooping, and clapping.

Alex saw Ms. Farmen glance down at her stopwatch and shake her head with slight disapproval.

When the applause had died down, Logan resumed, "So yeah. I'm running to be your president. I'll do my best. With all due respect for my worthy opponents, I think you should vote for me. Thanks, dudes!" He ended there, flashing double peace signs with both arms extended in a V, as the applause rose to thunderous levels. Then he ambled back to his seat and sat down, a sideways grin on his face.

Alex ignored the applause for Logan. She concentrated on Ms. Farmen, who was now quieting the audience in order to introduce her. The applause died down, and then when Ms. Farmen said her name, it swelled again, but not nearly as loudly as it had for Logan.

She floated to the microphone, unable to feel her feet. She felt oddly calm, her heart rate even, her hands dry as they held her carefully prepared remarks.

She lowered the microphone down a few inches—Logan was considerably taller than she was—and began.

"Good morning. My name is Alex Sackett, and I'm running for seventh-grade president. I had a speech prepared to deliver today." She held up her index cards. "I practiced it about a thousand times. But I'm not going to give that speech."

There was a murmur in the audience.

Alex's gaze came to rest on Ava, who was sitting, quietly listening.

"Instead I want to talk today about my twin sister, Ava. As most of you know, she has been prevented from joining the football team. The stated reason is that she might get hurt, but I think it's because she's a girl, and girls aren't supposed to play football. My worthy opponent here"—she gestured toward Logan, who gave the audience a cheerful thumbs-up—"has suggested that you might not want to vote for someone who's a—what did you call us, Logan? Rabble-rousers? Troublemakers?"

Logan gave another thumbs-up, and the audience roared with laughter.

"If that's what we Sacketts are, then I want to say how proud I am to be a Sackett."

Now you could hear a pin drop. Ms. Farmen had set down her stopwatch and her bell and was leaning forward to listen.

"I admit that for a while I felt ashamed and embarrassed that my sister wanted to play football. But now I feel proud of her. And indignant at the possibility that she will be unjustly prevented from doing what she loves. We're all in middle school. We all know how important it is to want to fit in, to be normal and accepted. But Ava has been true to herself. She doesn't care what people think of her. She is a hard worker. She is fiercely competitive. And she was born to play the game. Anyone going head-to-head with Ava Sackett is going to end up on the ground. Trust me—I lose every time there's a fight for our bathroom."

The crowd erupted with laughter.

"So whether you vote for me or not, I wanted to say that I'm proud to be a rabble-rouser, proud to stand up for what I really believe in, and proud to support someone really close to me who just wants to be herself. Thank you."

She heard a roaring in her ears as she took her seat and wasn't sure if it was applause or her own brain going weirdly haywire. As if through a fog, she heard Ms. Farmen introduce Ella, but Alex's gaze was fixed on Ava's face.

Ava was grinning. So what if Alex hadn't said anything about what she would do as president and had just torpedoed any possibility of getting herself elected? Ava was proud of her. And that was all that mattered.

CHAPTER FIFTEEN

Late Wednesday afternoon Ava stood in Alex's bedroom, wearing a skirt. A skirt. It belonged to Alex, of course, but she knew her twin wouldn't mind that she'd borrowed it. She hadn't seen Alex since the speech earlier that day. Alex and the other candidates had spent the lunch period in the teacher conference room, being interviewed by the staff at the school newspaper, the *Cub Reporter,* for a special online election edition that would come out the next day. And after school, Alex had gone to a debate club meeting, so Ava had come home by herself. She'd walked Moxy, eaten half a peanut butter sandwich, and then come upstairs to raid Alex's closet for a skirt.

"I look like Alex," she said out loud, as she gazed at her reflection in the mirror. Then she laughed, in spite of the several dozen butterflies flitting around inside her stomach. Of course she looked like Alex. But in a skirt, she *really* looked like her.

The school board was holding a special early meeting at six p.m. So Coach wouldn't be there, even if he had wanted to come. He rarely got out of practice before six. Ava swallowed. She understood why he wouldn't be coming with her.

He didn't want to be the focus of everyone's attention. He'd explained to her that this was her fight to fight, that he'd be thinking of her, that she needed to draw on all her grit and determination and stand up for what she believed in. And she'd told him she understood. But still, a tiny part of her wished he could be there.

A text came in from Jack.

Hey, good luck tonight.

Thanks. I'll need it.

Do you have to say
anything?

No, I hope not. I don't think so.

Well, maybe I'll see you.
I'm going to try to come.

Thanks.

I thought your sister's
speech was awesome.

I did, too.

CU

CU

Finally she heard her mother and Alex come in. She glanced at the clock. The meeting would start in one hour.

"I imagine there may be more people here tonight than at the usual school board meetings," said Mrs. Sackett, as they drove to the high school. Ava was sitting next to her, already uncomfortable in Alex's skirt. Its zipper was sticking painfully into her lower back.

Alex was sitting in the backseat. She'd insisted on coming along, and Ava was glad she was here. They'd even exchanged a big hug outside the bathroom just before they'd left. Ava had thanked her for her awesome speech.

"I just hope I lose to Ella, not Logan," Alex had told her.

"I'll try to park near the—" Mrs. Sackett broke off now, as she pulled into the high school parking lot.

"Wait. What's going on at the high school?" asked Alex.

The parking lot was a sea of cars.

"Mom?" asked Ava in a trembling voice.

"It looks like they're here for the meeting," said Mrs. Sackett. "I'll park over near the locker room area. We can try to get in through a side door."

But the side door was locked. The three of them traipsed toward the front of the high school. Just as they rounded the corner of the building, they heard someone say, "There she is!"

Ava was suddenly surrounded by news reporters thrusting microphones into her face. Bright lights flashed. Several people were asking her questions at the same time.

"Ava, how did you feel when you were told you couldn't play?"

"Ava! What does your father think about the possibility that you won't be allowed to play?"

"Hey, Ava! Look this way for a minute!"

Pop! Flash!

Ava felt her mother's arm around her waist. She was too short to see over the crowd of people mobbing her.

Suddenly a stern voice rang out. "Step aside, all of you! Let her proceed, please!"

It was Ms. Farmen, and she wasn't a principal for nothing. For such a small woman, she had the sort of voice people listened to. Meekly the reporters dropped away, and a path opened up for Ava, Alex, and their mother. Ava smiled gratefully at Ms. Farmen as they passed into the building. The principal was standing with her arms crossed and an expression on her face that could cut through steel. But she winked at Ava reassuringly.

The meeting had been moved from the library to the auditorium because of the size of the crowd that had turned up. But several dozen chairs had also been set up on the stage, and Mr. Guajardo, the head of the school board, gestured to them as they walked down the aisle that the Sacketts should sit up there. Ava noticed the Kellys were in the row a few behind theirs. Of course, she wasn't surprised to see them. She looked for Andy Baker out in the audience. There he was, sitting between what Ava assumed were his parents, in the second row of the auditorium.

Once they were settled in, Mr. Guajardo called the meeting to order, and then everyone stood up to pledge their allegiance to the flag. There was a roll call of board members, and then a motion to approve the proposed agenda.

Alex leaned across Ava to whisper to their mother. "When are they going to talk about Ava?"

"I think she's the last item on the agenda," Mrs. Sackett whispered back.

As the meeting droned on, Ava looked out at the people sitting in the audience and wondered if they were as bored as she was. She couldn't see if Jack was there but hoped for his sake that he wasn't.

The board discussed the annual review of the district's crisis and emergency management and medical emergency response plans. Ava's eyelids drooped. They discussed a proposal for another synthetic turf field at the high school. They discussed some calendar revision recommendations for the following school year. Ava's chin sagged toward her chest. They discussed renaming the band room at one of the elementary schools after a recently retired band teacher. Ava was pinching herself on the thigh so as not to drop off when she felt an elbow in her ribs. Her chin jerked back up and her eyes flew open.

"Our next item regards the advisability of permitting inter-gender participation on the Ashland Middle School football team," said Mr. Guajardo.

"You're next!" whispered her mom.

"But I won't have to say anything, right?" asked Ava.

"No," said her mom. "You just have to—"

"If we may ask Miss Ava Sackett to stand, please," said Mr. Guajardo.

The audience seemed to wake up from its collective dozing state. Ava shot her mother a horrified look as she stood up.

He looked up at Ava. "Is there anything you'd like to say to the board about your situation, Miss Sackett?"

"Um, no thanks," squeaked Ava. She sat back down. She wished again that Coach were there.

"Would anyone else care to say anything on this subject?" asked Mr. Guajardo.

There was a brief commotion on the stage behind Ava. She turned around. Mr. Kelly had risen to his feet.

"The board recognizes Mr. Kelly," said Mr. Guajardo.

Mr. Kelly took off his hat and held it against his chest. "I'd just like to say that with all due respect for this young lady, it is highly irregular for a girl to be permitted to play the great game of football."

Ava's mom had put her hand on Ava's arm, and now Ava felt her grip tighten.

Mr. Kelly went on. "There's a lot of rough contact, and a young lady might get injured, and the school district would be liable. There's no call for a girl to be playing a boys contact sport, and the law permits her to be prevented for her own good, given that there is an alternative sport offered, volleyball, which is much safer and more appropriate for young ladies. Thank you."

He put his hat back on and sat down.

Ava sprang back to her feet. "Actually, I would like to say something," she said.

Mr. Guajardo looked a bit surprised. "Very well. The board recognizes Miss Ava Sackett. You may proceed."

Ava swallowed. Her mouth had gone dry. Her heart was pounding. She did not like public speaking. Her anger and indignation had given her temporary courage, but now that courage drained away again. She looked at the members of the school board, who were all facing her, some with their hands folded in front of them, others with arms crossed—waiting. She looked out at all the people sitting in the audience.

And then she spotted Coach. He'd come after all! She could just make him out, silhouetted in the back doorway. She'd know his big, muscular frame anywhere. He must have slipped in so no one would see him. Her courage returned. She faced the board and spoke in a loud, clear voice.

"I've been playing football since I was three years old. I love the game. And my parents taught me the importance of fighting for what you believe in, the right way, with respect and persistence. And I don't believe it's fair to deny a kid the right to play a sport if she's good enough to make the team. Well, Coach K told me I was good enough, and that if I were a boy I would be on the team. So I'd like to please ask that you make the decision to let me play football."

Suddenly she became aware that Alex was now standing next to her.

"Mr. Guajardo, may I also say something?" asked Alex.

"The board recognizes Miss, er"—another board member leaned toward him and whispered something—"Miss Alexandra Sackett."

"Thank you," said Alex. "Ladies and gentlemen of the school board, my name is Alexandra Sackett, and I would like to say that it is unacceptable and unlawful to make a decision to bar a student from playing a sport based on her gender. This is a discriminatory policy and in clear violation of Title Nine, the 1972 federal law that mandates equal opportunities for men and women in education and athletics."

As Alex took a breath, Ava stared at her sister in wonder and admiration.

Alex went on. "As such, today I started an online petition requesting that Ashland Middle School allow Ava to play. As of this evening, we already had over eighteen hundred signatures, and they were still coming in fast when I left for tonight's meeting. I am sure the American Civil Liberties Union will take an interest in this decision if it doesn't go the way it rightfully should."

There was a murmur in the audience, and several camera flashes went off.

Ava linked her arm through Alex's, and the two sisters stood side by side.

Mr. Guajardo took off his glasses, and then put them back on. "Well!" he said. "Those were very impressive speeches from both of you. Thank you, Miss Sackett, and Miss Sackett, for your remarks. I move that we dismiss the spectators, media, and guests for our discussion. We will notify you of our decision tomorrow."

"Seconded," mumbled someone else.

"Please clear the auditorium now."

With that Mr. Guajardo banged his gavel. Immediately a crowd of reporters and parents and kids moved toward the stage. Ava turned to look at her mother.

"How do we get out of here?" she asked.

"Pssst! This way!" said a voice from offstage.

It was Jack Valdeavano, and he was beckoning to the Sacketts. Next to him were Coach, Tommy, and Kylie.

Quickly Ava, Alex, and Mrs. Sackett moved toward them, and they followed Jack backstage. They hurried through a dimly lit passageway and down some steps to a doorway with a lighted exit sign.

"You can get out this way," he said. "I don't think the reporters know about this stage door exit. My cousin is on the stage crew, and he showed me around recently. The parking lot will be just to your right, around the corner."

"Thank you so much!" said Mrs. Sackett.

"Thanks, Jack," said Ava.

"No problem. It's the least I could do. You guys were awesome," said Jack. "Now hurry up before they figure out where you've gone!"

"See you tomorrow!" said Kylie, giving Ava a big hug.

They got home ten minutes later, Mrs. Sackett and the girls in one car, Coach and Tommy in the other. Mrs. Sackett heated up the lentil soup she'd made earlier, and they all sat around the table.

"I'm proud of you girls," said Coach. "You stood up for what was right, and you stood up for each other. A parent can't ask for more than that."

"Yeah, you guys were pretty cool," agreed Tommy, ladling out the last of the soup into his bowl. "And I bet you'll be on the ten o'clock news."

They were.

CHAPTER SIXTEEN

Thursday morning, as their bus pulled into the unloading area at school, Ava looked out the window to see a crowd of reporters.

"Oh no," she said, nudging Alex and pointing outside.

"Wow," said Alex. "They're certainly making a big deal out of this."

As they stood up to file off, Ava put a hand on her sister's shoulder. "Hey, Al? Thanks for your speeches yesterday and last night."

Alex smiled. "It took me a while to get a clue, but I guess you're used to that by now."

Ava saw with relief that Ms. Farmen was standing at the door of the bus, ready to escort

Alex and Ava into the school. "We'll let you know when the school board's decision has been announced," she said to the reporters. "Now please let these children enter their school so that learning may commence."

Once again, the reporters meekly dropped away.

As they moved down the hallway toward their lockers, Alex pointed at the walls. "Look!" she said. "With all the football excitement, I totally forgot today was election day!"

Someone had put up dozens of new posters advertising Alex's campaign. Every few feet was another sign.

"'She's five foot two and the president for you!'" Ava read. "'Check the bracket next to Sackett!' These are great! Who do you think did them?"

"I'm guessing it was Emily and Lindsey," said Alex, smiling.

"I'm going to go vote," said Ava. "Good luck today, Al."

"Thanks, Ava," said Alex. "Good luck today to you, too. I hope they let you go to practice."

Ava was about to go into homeroom when Ms. Kerry intercepted her in the doorway. "You're supposed to report directly to Ms. Farmen's office," she said to Ava. "Good luck."

Ava thanked her, and a few minutes later Mrs. Gusman was escorting her into Ms. Farmen's office. Coach Kenerson and Mr. Guajardo were also there. They stood up when she came in.

"Sit down, Ava," said Ms. Farmen. "This will be brief, as I know you need to get to class. Mr. Guajardo?"

"First off, Miss Sackett," said Mr. Guajardo, "I would like to commend you, and your sister, for the way you conducted yourselves at the meeting last night. The board was very impressed with your poise, your perseverance, and the respectful way that you presented your case."

"Thanks," said Ava, her voice barely above a whisper. Her heart was pounding with anticipation.

"The board has decided that it will allow you to remain a member of the Ashland Middle School football team."

Ava leaped up and shrieked. "That's totally awesome!" she said. "Thank you so much!"

Coach Kenerson was beaming. "Told him you're my best kicker," he said. "I'm going to move Xander to punter and have you be our field goal kicker. You've got an excellent foot. And I want you to train with the receivers, too, Sackett. You've got good hands."

"Receivers?" repeated Ava, dumbfounded. "I've never played that position."

"You had the second-fastest time in the pro-agility test," said Coach K. "And a four-point-nine-five-second forty. I'd be foolish not to use your speed and quickness."

"All right, Ava, you may go to class now," said Ms. Farmen, rising from her chair. Everyone else stood up too. "Congratulations."

Ava shook hands quickly with all three of them and then practically danced her way to Spanish class.

Alex was just setting up her science lab with Madison when Ava's text came in, telling her about the football decision. She knew, of course, that she wasn't allowed to use her phone in class, but today she didn't care if she got in trouble. She'd told Ava she wanted to be the first to hear.

She inhaled sharply when she looked at her phone.

"What's up?" asked Madison, who was lining up their beakers.

"Alex?" Mr. Lehner was across the room, helping Ella Sanchez and her partner, Nate Nielson, adjust a Bunsen burner. He peered at her through his safety goggles, looking a bit like a fish in an aquarium. "Something to share with the group? I'm sure you weren't texting, right?"

"Um, well, maybe just a tiny bit," said Alex, flushing. "You can give me a detention for it, Mr. Lehner, but I had to know what the school board decided about my sister."

"Well, tell us then!" said Mr. Lehner. The rest of the class stopped what they were doing at their lab tables and all waited to hear what Alex was going to say.

"They're going to let her play!" said Alex, bouncing up and down with excitement.

The class erupted in a cheer. Alex was pleased to see that even Ella looked genuinely delighted.

After science class, as Alex was packing up her stuff, Ella Sanchez made her way over to her.

"Hey, Alex, can I talk to you for a minute?" she asked shyly.

"Sure!" said Alex, trying to hide her surprise. She and Ella had never really had a conversation before now. And on election day, of all days!

"I just wanted to tell you that I think your speech yesterday was really great," said Ella. "I'm really happy for your sister. And if I don't win this dumb election, I hope you do. The worst scenario would be if Logan won."

Alex smiled. "I agree! I have a sinking feeling he's going to win because he's so popular. Plus, I don't think my speech that was all about my sister necessarily helped my candidacy. But I really appreciate your saying that, and I think you'd make a great president."

"Well, between you and me," said Ella, lowering her voice, "I honestly won't be devastated if I lose. My parents are the ones who pushed me to run. My mom practically wrote my speech, and my dad's secretary make all those fancy signs. I would rather just hang out at the science lab and work on my experiments. But they think I need to be well-rounded for when I apply to college. Which won't even happen for five more years."

Alex laughed. "Thanks for telling me, Ella," she said.

"I'll walk you toward S wing," said Ella. "I want to float an idea past you, if you're free after school today."

CHAPTER SEVENTEEN

Thursday afternoon Ava emerged from the girls' locker room in her helmet and full pads. The girls in the locker room from the volleyball and cross-country teams had all high-fived her and congratulated her. She was happy the whole controversy was over and just wanted things to get back to normal so she could concentrate on football.

"Hey, Sackett," said a voice as she passed the boys' locker room. She turned. It was Xander, also wearing his practice uniform and pads. His helmet was under his arm.

"I just wanted to say congratulations on making the team," he said, his eyes cast down.

"Thanks. You too. I'm sure you'll be an awesome punter," she said.

"I'm going to be a lineman, too," he said, and Ava could hear the pride in his voice. "So, um, I also wanted to say I was sorry," he said in a low voice.

"For what?"

"I'm the one who stuck that picture in your locker. It was dumb. I was just afraid, well, afraid of what people would say if I got cut from the team, beaten out by a girl."

Ava nodded. "I get it," she said. "But I wish people would stop looking at me like a girl who plays football, and just look at me as a football player."

"Yeah, well, you mow down enough guys, they'll forget pretty quickly," he said.

Ava grinned at him. "I hope so," she said.

The two walked up to join the rest of the team. For the warm-up run, Ava noticed that Xander pointedly ran next to her, rather than with Andy. After the run, the captains told Ava to move to the front line for stretching.

CHAPTER EIGHTEEN

On Friday morning Alex woke up early, feeling strangely calm. Today was the day they were going to announce the election results. So why wasn't she a nervous wreck? She felt similar to the way she felt after she had handed in an important test. The studying and test-taking were the stressful parts. After you handed it in, there was nothing more you could do to change anything. It was the same with the election. The votes were cast and counted. Whatever happened, happened.

The morning breakfast rush felt lighter and less stressful than it had in some time. Alex and Ava were getting along again. With the whirlwind of speeches, and the school board meeting, and football practice, and Alex's errand with Ella Sanchez the day before, the twins hadn't had a chance to have a real talk, but the tension was gone. Ava was happy and excited about football. Alex was relieved that the election was over, come what may.

Just before lunch, everyone filed into the auditorium for an all-school assembly to announce the election results. Alex wished she could sit with Ava, but you were supposed to sit with your fourth-period class, and that, ironically, was gym for Alex. Not her best subject. The only person she kind of knew in the class was Madison.

Ms. Farmen droned on for a few minutes about fall Homecoming and the upcoming all-school community service day. Then at last she cleared her throat. "And now, we turn to the results of the all-school elections. Starting with sixth grade."

She opened one of the envelopes in front of her and read off the results of class secretary, treasurer, vice president, and president. Chloe Klein got president and received an enthusiastic round of applause and whoops. She stood up and waved, grinning broadly.

Alex held her breath while Ms. Farmen

opened the next envelope. She felt Madison grab her hand and squeeze it rather painfully. Ms. Farmen read off the names of the secretary, treasurer, and vice president, each announcement followed by applause.

"And the winner of the presidential election for this year's seventh-grade class is"—she paused dramatically—"Alex Sackett!"

The place erupted. Alex felt like she was dreaming. She felt Madison gently guide her up to a standing position, and she stood up and waved to the crowd.

Ava and Kylie, about ten seats in front and to the right of her, were going crazy. Corey was over on the left aisle with a big group of his football teammates, and they were standing up and clapping and whistling. Emily and Lindsey were jumping up and down and cheering.

She couldn't see Ella or Logan. She'd look for Ella later.

She couldn't believe it. She'd actually won.

Ava's first game was at home on Saturday morning; the Tiger Cubs were playing the Mainville

Hawks. She dressed alone in the quiet girls' locker room. Next door she could hear her teammates yelling and getting psyched. It was strange not to be in the midst of all that, but she'd get used to it.

She walked over to the field in her uniform— number fourteen—and she saw Alex waiting for her near the chain-link fence just behind their bench. As she trotted toward her sister, her eye was drawn to something else. A sea of pink in the stands. Even Alex was wearing a pink shirt, and Alex rarely wore pink.

"Hey, Ave! You like our shirts?" asked Alex, her eyes shining, as Ava got closer.

Ava looked. Alex took a step back so she could read what it said on the front of her pink T-shirt. There was a silhouette of a girl football player and above it, the words GIRLS CAN'T WHAT? Then Alex turned around so Ava could see the back. SACKETT #14.

"Where did these come from?" asked Ava, her eye moving toward the stand. She realized that at least half the spectators—and practically all the middle-school-aged kids—had the shirt on.

"Ella Sanchez," said Alex. "She was totally psyched about you being able to play, and we met with her dad on Thursday and he offered to help us get these T-shirts made. That's where I went yesterday afternoon, too—to his printing company. He got half his staff to drop what they were doing so we could get them done in time for the game! They finished them late last night. Ella's handing them out at the entrance— you wouldn't believe how enthusiastic people are about wearing them!"

Ava felt her eyes mist up and was glad she had her helmet on. She was not going to be seen crying at her first game. She gave her sister a quick hug.

"Thanks, Al. I'm the luckiest sister in the world."

"Go win the game!" said Alex, with a tap on Ava's helmet.

Ava grinned and went to join her team.

Alex was climbing the bleachers toward where her mom sat when Emily and Lindsey jumped up from their seats to give her a huge hug. They were both wearing pink shirts too.

"So what did Charlie say when you told him you'd won?" asked Lindsey.

"Charlie?" said Alex, furrowing her brow.

"Yeah! Charlie!"

Alex was about to ask who in the world Charlie was when she remembered, in the nick of time, that Charlie was her pretend boyfriend from back home—the name she'd blurted out to them as a way to avoid complications with Corey.

"Oh! Ah, right! He's psyched, ha-ha," she replied. *That was a close one,* she thought. "Well! I'd better get going. It's almost game time!"

Coach and Tommy joined Alex and Mrs. Sackett just as Ava kicked off to start the game. All four Sacketts were wearing the pink T-shirts.

"Awesome idea, Alex," said Coach, giving her a quick hug. "I'm proud of my girls."

"Thanks, Daddy," said Alex.

"Do you think he'll try her at receiver today?" asked Mrs. Sackett.

"I doubt it," said Coach. "She hasn't been practicing with the team enough. Probably needs another week or two to learn the plays. But that was a fine kickoff."

"Look, Daddy!" whispered Alex. "There are the Kellys over there."

Sure enough, Mr. and Mrs. Kelly were sitting

a few rows in front of the Sacketts. The Kellys were conspicuous for being among the few Ashland fans not wearing pink T-shirts. Their arms were crossed primly in front of them.

"Why are they even here?" Alex hissed.

"Ava says they have a nephew on the team," said Mrs. Sackett.

Alex forgot about the Kellys in the excitement of the game.

At the end of the first half, the score was 7–6 after Corey found Andy Baker in the end zone for a fifteen-yard touchdown pass. The Tiger Cubs had the chance to kick the extra point, but Coach K signaled them to attempt a two-point conversion. The runner, Owen Rooney, was buried at the one yard line.

"Why didn't he let Ava try to kick it?" demanded Mrs. Sackett.

"Because Coach K wanted to get ahead," said Coach. "It could end up being a low-scoring game. With only two touchdowns in the first half, he went for two points rather than one."

With five minutes to play in the third quarter, the score was still 7–6. Ava finally trotted onto the field with the field goal kicking team. It was a twenty-one-yard attempt.

The Ashland spectators rose to their feet and cheered.

The center snapped the ball to Corey. Ava took one step with her left, planted her right foot, swung back wide, and booted the ball.

It soared through the goal posts and the crowd went wild. The scoreboard read 9–7.

Alex glanced over at the Kellys. They remained seated, arms still crossed disapprovingly.

But by the time the clock ticked down in the final seconds, Ava's team was still ahead 9–7. Ava's kick had proved the decisive factor in the win. Now the fans in pink were back on their feet, roaring and cheering "Ayyy-VAH! Ayyy-VAH! Ayy-VAH!"

Alex glanced at the Kellys once more. Mrs. Kelly was on her feet and had joined in the chant. Mr. Kelly was still slumped in his seat, stoic and immovable. As Alex watched, Mrs. Kelly turned and bashed her husband over the head with her rolled-up program.

"Oh, stand up, Doug!" Alex heard Mrs. Kelly say. "That girl can kick!"

Alex turned back toward the scoreboard just as it ticked down to zero. Ava's team had won.

Alex smiled. Yep. That girl really could kick.

Ready for more
ALEX AND AVA?

Here's a sneak peek at the next
book in the It Takes Two series:

Go! Fight!
Twin!

Bam! Bam! Bam! Bam!

The bass drum player was pounding
rhythmically to excite the crowd. The cheerleaders
shouted and clapped and performed hair-raising
acrobatics. Ava Sackett watched, holding her
breath, as her friend Kylie McClaire's older sister,
Yvette, stood on another girl's shoulders high
above the ground and then pointed one leg up
into the air.

But then the opposing team scored another
field goal, and the Ashland Tigers' fans lapsed
into a despondent silence. The Tigers were
losing by seventeen points, and there were only
seven minutes left in the game.

From her seat high in the stands, Ava looked down at her older brother, Tommy. He stood on the sidelines with the rest of his teammates, dejectedly watching what was happening on the field. His helmet was off, and when he turned his head, she could see his thick brown hair drooping down over his eyes. Ava knew what he was thinking—not only was the team going to lose, but also there was no way he'd be going into the game.

Farther along the sideline was their father, Mike Sackett, who was the coach of the Ashland Tigers. His job was the reason their family had moved to Ashland, Texas, from the East Coast just a few months earlier. Ava watched as Coach stalked up and down the sideline in his Tigers jacket, communicating with his assistant coaches through the big headphones he wore. The assistant coaches were stationed in the tower high above the field, where they could watch the game.

The crowd groaned.

"What happened?" demanded Ava's friend Kylie. Kylie hadn't really paid attention to football before she and Ava became friends—she was more interested in things like jewelry making and fantasy novels—but Ava was teaching her how the game worked. To Ava's delight, Kylie seemed to enjoy football almost as much as Ava did.

"PJ misjudged the throw," said Ava. "Did you see how Tyler Whitley stopped and cut over toward the sideline? PJ's lucky it didn't get intercepted. It doesn't look good."

"Is there any way we can pull out a win?" asked Kylie.

"Highly doubtful." Ava watched Kylie's sister leap off two people's shoulders, land in a pike on their waiting arms, bounce up onto her feet, do a backbend, and finally land in a split. "Wow. Your sister is awesome."

"Wow. Kylie McClaire's sister is awesome," said Alex Sackett, who was sitting between Lindsey Davis and Emily Campbell, a few feet farther along the bleacher from her twin sister.

"She's amazing," agreed Emily.

Alex watched in fascination as Yvette stood on the shoulders of two teammates standing side by side, her arms up in a V. Then she pulled her right leg up from the side so it was touching her ear—all while standing on one foot on someone's shoulder.

"She's so flexible," said Alex.

"Well, at our level we don't do stuff like that," said Lindsey. "But we do a lot of choreographed routines. It just takes practice."

"I'm sure you could do it if you worked at it, Alex," said Emily. "You should try out for cheerleading with us."

"Yeah," agreed Lindsey. "You're from such an athletic family."

"Ha," said Alex. "Ava and Tommy inherited all the athletic genes." Not only was Tommy on the high school football team, but Ava had just made the middle school football team a few weeks ago. Alex noticed that Rosa Navarro, sitting on the other side of Lindsey, was listening intently to the conversation but not adding to it. Alex had heard Rosa was one of the best seventh grade cheerleaders. *Does she not think I have what it takes?* Alex wondered.

"It's a combination of dance, gymnastics, and tumbling," Emily said. "But not all of us do the big acrobatic tumbling stuff. That you really do need to have practiced from a young age."

"Rosa's our best tumbler," said Lindsey.

"Don't you think Alex should try out, Rosa?" asked Emily.

Rosa hesitated. "Well, not everyone is cut out for cheerleading," she said. "It takes a lot of coordination and flexibility."

Alex's eyes narrowed. What was that supposed to mean? Did Rosa think she was uncoordinated?

The roar of the opposing team's fans interrupted the conversation. The clock ran down. The Tigers had lost.

Alex was still busy thinking as everyone stood up to leave and her sister poked her arm.

"That was pretty grim," said Ava.

"Huh? What was grim?" asked Alex, puzzled.

Ava stared at her. "Uh, the game? The fact that we just lost?"

"Oh!" said Alex with a little laugh. "Right. Yeah, too bad. So are you going to Sal's?" The middle school kids usually gathered at the local pizza place after home games.

Ava frowned at her. "Yeah, I promised Kylie I'd head over with her," she said. "But I'm only staying for a little while—I want to rest up for my game tomorrow. I'll see you there?"

"Yep, sure," said Alex. She was still thinking

about Rosa's remarks. Not that she had time to participate in sports, now that she was class president. And it was true that Alex herself commented all the time that she was uncoordinated athletically. But it was one thing for Alex to say it. It was quite another thing for someone else to agree with her, out loud, in front of everyone.

And honestly, cheerleading? How hard could it be?

Belle Payton isn't a twin herself, but she does have twin brothers! She spent much of her childhood in the bleachers reading–er, cheering them on–at their football games. Though she left the South long ago to become a children's book editor in New York City, Belle still drinks approximately a gallon of sweet tea a week and loves treating her friends to her famous homemade mac-and-cheese. Belle is the author of many books for children and tweens, and is currently having a blast writing two sides to each It Takes Two story.